AMERICAN FOLK

AMERICAN FOLK
CLASSIC TALES RETOLD

by Charles Sullivan

Illustrated by Warren Infield

Harry N. Abrams, Inc., Publishers

A portion of the proceeds from the sale of this book will be contributed to
The American Foundation for the Arts.

PROJECT MANAGER: Elisa Urbanelli
EDITOR: Julia Gaviria
DESIGNER: Darilyn Lowe Carnes

Library of Congress Cataloging-in-Publication Data

Sullivan, Charles, 1933–
       American folk : classic tales retold / Charles Sullivan ; illustrations by
   Warren Infield.
          p.   cm.
       ISBN 0–8109–0655–4
       1. Tales—United States.   I. Title.
   GR105.S86   1998
   398.2'0973—dc21   98–6191

Printed and bound in Japan

 Harry N. Abrams, Inc.
100 Fifth Avenue
New York, N.Y. 10011
www.abramsbooks.com

This book is dedicated to my darling wife,

Shirley Ross Sullivan,

the bright lady of my sonnets.

TABLE OF CONTENTS

OTHER COLORFUL CHARACTERS

INCREDIBLE ANIMALS

INTRODUCTION

American folk tales come in many shapes and sizes. They can be plain or fancy, happy or sad, funny or scary, lyrical or down-to-earth, obvious or mysterious, believable or outlandish, easy to follow or hard to understand. They range in length from a few sentences about a single character to complicated stories that would take hours to tell or to read. Like the American people themselves, each is at least a little bit different from the others.

In spite of this great variety among American folk tales, I find that the most interesting ones fall into five general categories: (1) tales about characters who are larger than life, such as John Henry or Pocahontas; (2) tales about outlaws, crooks, and cheaters, such as the Petticoat Pirates or Jesse James; (3) tales about heroines and heroes, such as Elfrego Baca or Molly Brown; (4) tales about other kinds of colorful characters, such as Calamity Jane or Johnny Appleseed; and (5) tales about incredible animals, such as Br'er Rabbit or Two-Toe Tom, the Giant Alligator. This book is organized accordingly.

Americans have always been fond of folk tales whose characters are larger than life. Among those presented in Chapter One, John Henry the construction worker and Davy Crockett the frontiersman have more physical strength and determination than ordinary human beings, although they are all too human themselves. Joe Magarac, man of steel, has superhuman capabilities that he uses for the benefit of others. The giant Paul Bunyan and his equally gigantic companion, the blue ox "Babe," remind us that in folk tales, animals too can be larger than life. Some tales depict a character that is not just stronger or smarter than normal, but distinct from most humans in some mysterious way. For example, magical properties are possessed by Pecos Bill, who knows how to make ferocious animals do his bidding. The character who calls himself Kilroy also has magical, almost mythical powers—he is able to be in different places at the same time. Other characters such as Uncle Sam and the Native American princess Pocahontas are as much mythical as human, although they may have originated with real people. In the tale of the River God's wife, we see people relating themselves to a mythical figure in the course of their everyday lives. And a special category of characters larger than life includes the tales of political leaders whose virtuous deeds commend them to generation after generation of Americans. George Washington's confession to his father, Abe Lincoln's proverbial honesty, and Teddy Roosevelt's refusal to shoot a little bear are three favorites.

Outlaws, crooks, and cheaters appear in many American folk tales. Sometimes we may be tickled by their cleverness, provided they do no great harm to others. Examples in Chapter Two include Black Bart, the schoolteacher turned stagecoach robber who writes poetry, a quick-thinking widow who outsmarts Jesse James, two female pirates who sometimes dress up in petticoats, the nameless Ozark mountaineer who matches wits with a sophisticated Arkansas traveler, and Steve Brodie, the bold young fellow who claims he has jumped off the Brooklyn Bridge. In other tales—for instance, Judge Roy Bean and his pet bear, the plan to saw off Manhattan from the rest of New York, and the endless herd of cattle—a crook or cheater who tries to be clever is foiled by someone more clever or more fortunate. Then we find characters caught up in tragic situations, so that we tend to forgive their misdeeds, as in the tales of Frankie & Johnnie and Captain Kidd. On the other hand, some outlaws, crooks, and cheaters are justly punished, such as Colonel Plug, the riverboat wrecker, and the young desperado known as Billy the Kid.

Heroines and heroes, those unusual women and men who demonstrate great courage at moments of danger, are popular folk characters. In fact it appears that American women achieved equality of recognition earlier in folk tales than they did in more "literary" forms of literature, such as novels or plays. Among the examples presented in Chapter Three, we see a young black woman escaping from slavery by crossing a frozen river, her baby in her arms. Molly Pitcher performs heroically in the American Revolution, as does the elderly Barbara Frietchie during the Civil War. The historic expedition of Lewis and Clark is successful because a young Native American woman guides them through the trackless wilderness. And the legendary Molly Brown emerges as a heroine from the catastrophic sinking of the ocean liner *Titanic*. Some of the traditional male characters show their heroism in combat, when they are greatly outnumbered. For instance, one young Texas Ranger proves that he is equal to an unruly crowd. Elfrego Baca, the fearless deputy sheriff, shoots his way out of a jail surrounded by outlaws. Henrik Van Wempel, a businessman beset by thieves, overcomes them with the help of his angry goose. In the realm of mythology, a young Native American brave named Cloud-Carrier defies the mightiest warrior of the Star Folk. Other characters are elevated to heroism by a crisis or emergency—for example, Columbus in his voyage through the "sea of gloom" to America, the pirate Jean Lafitte at the battle of New Orleans, and Casey Jones, who dies in a train wreck to spare the lives of fellow workers.

Colorful characters of various other kinds are found in American folk tales. They may appear to have little in common, but most of them are pursuing their personal dreams. For example, in Chapter Four, Rosie the Riveter wants to do more than stay home and knit sweaters as her country enters World War II. Out in the Wild West, a young man tries to outdo his bronco-busting father, Billy Earthquake. A penniless but talented young woman becomes the Cinderella of Santa Fe, New Mexico. Back East, Rip Van Winkle dreams his way into the past, while Ponce de Léon seeks eternal youth, and early Viking explorers search for a whole new world despite the hardships of their journey. One of the most intriguing folk characters, Johnny Appleseed, dreams of providing abundance for everyone, in contrast to Ichabod Crane, whose fantasies of love are forgotten after a nightmarish encounter with a headless horseman. Other folk characters go wandering across America to find something—they include Windwagon Thomas the landlocked sailor, sweet Betsey from Pike, and a young man who drops out of Yale University and becomes a sheepherder. An endearing but melancholy character whose dreams of love come to an early end is Calamity Jane.

Incredible animals hop, gallop, fly, swim, or crawl through folk tales, including some that have their origins in African-American stories, such as Br'er Rabbit and Br'er Fox or Compair Bouki and the monkeys, presented in Chapter Five. Sometimes a mean or scary animal turns out to be friendly, like the goat that sees red or Two-Toe Tom, the giant alligator. More often, the animal is a creature that somebody hopes to exploit or take advantage of—for example, the gollywhopper, the giant catfish, the jumping frog, the fur-bearing trout, or the groundhog that sees his shadow. Rarely are humans harmed by incredible animals, even those as big as Crook-jaw the whale or as hungry as a pack of wolves. Occasionally, for instance in the tale of Daniel Boone and the deer, an animal leads a human mysteriously towards a deeper appreciation of life in the natural world.

To round out this collection of sixty American folk tales, each chapter ends with some brief notes about additional examples, including other familiar favorites as well as lesser-known tales that are hard to find.

What makes these folk tales different from other kinds of stories? Two things come to mind. First, they generally emphasize some of the most positive values in American life. Love, kindness and generosity, resourcefulness and creativity, courage in the face of danger, and eagerness to meet challenges—one or another of these qualities will usually come out on top as the tale ends. Even with this positive emphasis, however, many folk characters walk a crooked line between right and wrong. They tend to have a strong sense of independence, of being free from rules and restrictions, going beyond the limits of what is normally possible or permissible. Thus a folk character may be bigger, braver, stronger, smarter, more talented than other people—but he or she may also be less law-abiding, less honest, less fair. Writers and tellers of folk tales are often willing to take a risk, to turn such extraordinary characters loose among more conventional ones, just to see what happens.

The second thing that differentiates folk tales from other kinds of stories is the writing or telling itself. Literature usually has authors, but the creators of folk tales are usually anonymous. The stories don't belong to anyone in particular—they are passed along from one person to another, and in this process it is expected that they will be changed. Even in exceptional cases, where authors have put their names on folk tales, this rule of change still holds true. For example, Samuel Clemens (who made himself into a folk character named Mark Twain) changed the story of the jumping frog when he borrowed it from an old newspaper. Joel Chandler Harris altered some of the African tales he heard about Br'er Rabbit and Br'er Fox in the American South. A really amazing example of creative change is the tale of John Henry, which has counterparts in so many different places that nobody can be sure when or where or how it originated.

In this spirit of telling and retelling, I have felt free to take American folk tales from wherever I found them or heard them, and to retell them yet again, sometimes sticking close to an earlier version, sometimes making changes that I hope will result in better stories. In search of tales to read or listen to, I have traveled the length and breadth of America and have become more fond and proud of my fabulous country—despite its imperfections—because of its boundless humanity. Though many American folk tales take us back to earlier times, the values they reflect and the problems they pose can still be found today, and will be with us, our children, and our grandchildren tomorrow.

Charles Sullivan
McLean, Virginia, and
San Francisco, California

CHARACTERS LARGER THAN LIFE

John Henry Never Quits

John Henry Davidson lived with his mother, his father, and his grandfather in the peaceful town of Fairmont, West Virginia, until he went off to college at Virginia Tech. He was a tall, strapping fellow, with a chemistry book in one hand and a tennis racquet in the other, and he seemed destined to do great things. But his story really began when he was just six years old, coming home from school in tears after his first day in the first grade. His parents were both working. His grandfather, recently retired from a job with the state highway department, sat waiting for him on the shady front porch of their white frame house.

"What's the trouble, John Henry?" his grandfather asked.

"The trouble is my name, Grandpa," the little boy sniffed. "Some of the older kids are making fun of me because I call myself John Henry, like the song."

"But you *are* John Henry," his grandfather exclaimed. "Same as your daddy and same as me. I was there when they named you."

"Oh, you know what I mean, Grandpa," the boy replied. "I'm not the real John Henry, I'm not big and strong, and the boys are making jokes about me."

"Come sit for a while," said his grandfather. "Tell me what you know about the real John Henry."

"Well, like the song says, he was a steel-driving man. He worked on a tunnel somewhere around here."

"And what does that mean exactly, calling sonebody a steel-driving man?" his grandfather continued.

"I don't really know," the boy admitted.

"Would you like me to tell you?"

"I sure would, Grandpa."

So the grandfather got two glasses of milk from the kitchen, and a plate of his favorite biscuits, and they sat on the porch while he told his grandson the tale.

"The real John Henry was a working man, first of all—big and strong, but not the biggest, maybe not even the strongest. Yet he had some kind of pride inside of him—John Henry just couldn't stand to see any man, black or white, work harder or faster than he did."

"He was black," the boy said.

"He was black, sure enough, like you and me, but everyone respected him for what he could do. When it came right down to work, pure and simple, the color of a man's skin didn't make a whole lot of difference."

"So what was the steel-driving part?" the boy asked.

"Well," said his grandfather, "just picture what they were trying to do—more than a hundred years ago. Here was this new railroad being built, and here was this mountain. The railroad couldn't go over the mountain or around the mountain, the railroad had to go through it."

"And the mountain was solid rock," said the boy.

"Solid rock, that's right, and in those days there wasn't all the heavy equipment they use now. They had to blast their way through that old mountain—blast and shovel, blast and shovel, one or two feet a day—going at it from both ends and hoping they would meet in the middle."

"Did John Henry do the blasting?" the boy said.

"No, John Henry made the holes to put the blasting powder in. He hit a long steel bar with a sledgehammer, over and over again, and inch by inch that steel was driven deeper and deeper into the rock—maybe ten or twelve feet for each hole, to make it deep enough. Then other men would put the blasting powder in several holes at once, and light the fuses, and run back out of the tunnel, and—"

"Wham!" the boy exclaimed.

"Wham is right," his grandfather agreed. "The noise was so loud, you'd think the whole mountain had exploded, and everything was covered with dust. But when they went back in to shovel out the pieces, there wasn't all that much to shovel."

"Then John Henry would have to make more holes?" the boy said, "Driving the steel again?"

"Exactly right. Other men drove steel too, of course, but John Henry could drive it harder and faster than anybody else, working ten or twelve hours a day."

"Like the song says, Grandpa, he was the best in the land."

"He surely tried to be. He worked so hard he broke some of the sledgehammers. He wore out those bars of steel—bent them or twisted them or broke off the points—and he wore out the men who held them in place for him while he swung the hammer. If John Henry wasn't the best in the land, nobody could tell him the name of any man who was better."

"But then something happened," the boy said.

"That's right. One day John Henry's boss asked him to compete against a steam-drill, a new invention that might someday take the place of men swinging hammers and driving steel."

"Was the steam-drill like an electric drill, that you could hold in your hand?" the boy asked.

"No, this was a big old thing, with all kinds of pipes and boilers, and a steam-hose attached to a drill so heavy that most men couldn't even pick it up."

"What happened, Grandpa?"

"Well, the men from the steam-drill company heated up about a hundred gallons of water to make steam for the drill, and when it was ready John Henry and the steam-drill man, a white man, shook hands. Then they took their positions facing the rock, about ten feet apart, side by side, ready to start."

"Then what happened?"

"The boss just yelled at them to go, and off they went. At first the steam-drill was doing better than John Henry. It went about four feet into the rock, while John Henry hadn't gone but a foot or two. A lot of the men who had bet on John Henry were wishing they could put their money on the steam-drill instead, but of course it was too late. When John Henry saw that he was falling behind, he stopped and asked his boss a favor."

"A favor!" the boy cried. "What kind of favor?"

"John Henry wanted to know if he could use two sledgehammers at once, left hand and right, so he could drive the steel twice as fast. Nobody had ever done that before, but his boss said okay, so that's what John Henry did."

"Bam with the left! Bam with the right!" the boy exclaimed.

"Yes, indeed. So John Henry caught up with the steam-drill, little by little. Then it seemed like the drill was running out of steam—it huffed and puffed, but didn't go nearly as fast as before."

"Then what happened?"

"The drill stopped. So John Henry just stopped and waited while they heated up another hundred gallons of water to make more steam. Then the drill started up again, and John Henry started too. But sometime later he began to feel dizzy. He needed water himself, but the steam-drill man wouldn't stop and wait for him to drink it, so

15

he just kept on going. He got so dry he wasn't even sweating any more, though he was working very hard and the day was hot. Some of the men told him to slow down, to quit, but you know what he did?"

"He just kept going," the boy said, "and he won."

"Yes he did, and the steam-drill people were so embarrassed they took their equipment back to the factory, to try and improve it."

"What ever happened to that old steam-drill?" the boy wondered.

"I don't rightly know, but I don't believe it was ever used again."

"And what happened to John Henry?" the boy asked. "He died, didn't he?"

"Yes he did—not right away, but a few hours later, back in the bunkhouse where he had lived with the other men. He died quietly, without saying anything to anybody. Maybe a heart attack. Anyway, they gave him as big a funeral as they could, the following Sunday. People came from all over West Virginia and other places even farther away, to pay their respects."

"Were you there, Grandpa?"

"No, but my daddy was. His name was Chester Davidson. I was born not long after that, and given the name of John Henry."

"And then my father, and then me," said the boy.

"That's right," his grandfather agreed. "Now let me ask you something—are you going back to school tomorrow and cry about your name?"

"No," the boy said slowly, "I don't think so."

"Well, then, what are you going to do?"

"I'm going to do what the real John Henry did—I mean that other John Henry, 'cause I'm a real one too. I'm going to figure out some way that I can be the best in the land."

"That's fine," his grandfather smiled.

"But you know what, Grandpa? If that old steam-drill runs out of steam this time, I'm not going to stop and wait for it. I'm going to keep right on driving that steel!"

Davy Crockett Goes to Washington

Davy Crockett liked nothing better than a good fight, the way other people like sports or just plain exercise, but when he was elected to Congress in 1827 by the voters of western Tennessee, he figured he'd better act more like a gentleman. At least to start with. So Davy bought the largest black suit he could find, cut off some of his tangled hair with a hunting knife, and left his long rifle at home when he set out on foot for the city of Washington, D.C.

He was thinking about politics as he strode lightly through the forest, not paying attention as he should have. Suddenly he found himself surrounded by dozens of Indian braves wearing war paint, carrying tomahawks, and pointing muskets at him.

Thirty or forty against one! What a fight that could be! Davy let out a whoop of joy, startling his captors for a moment, but he didn't attack them because he might have ruined his new clothes. As he hesitated the crowd parted and another Indian appeared, a man so big that Davy felt small for the first time since childhood. He was dressed like the others in winter buckskins but he carried no weapons, only a law book that looked familiar to the puzzled backwoodsman.

"Congressman Crockett, I presume," he said in English much better than Davy's own. "Allow me to introduce myself."

Davy learned that the enormous Indian was a hereditary chieftain, who used the name Pericles Eubanks when it was necessary for him to deal with whites. He had earned degrees in theology and law at Georgetown College, and now he was back among his people to help protect their interests.

"Do you intend to represent us in Washington," he asked Davy, "as well as your own kind?"

Davy was wondering if he could possibly beat this young giant in a wrestling match, just the two of them, but he heard the question and answered yes. Eubanks then explained that his tribe had been cheated out of land that was rightfully theirs, between the Tennessee River and the Mississippi in Crockett's own district.

"I'd get hung if I tried to give any land back to these Indians," Davy thought. "But what the heck? I guess I'm their Congressman too, so I'll listen."

"Let me have your story," he said aloud.

"In the time before time," Eubanks began, "when He Who Is Sky came to visit She Who Is Earth—"

Davy tried to interrupt, but Eubanks insisted on telling it in the traditional way. Sky, earth, more sky, big rains, then lakes and rivers, sun shining, people born, people not trying to own the earth on which they were allowed to live.

"How's that again?" said Davy. "Why right there in your law book—"

"Indian laws are different," Eubanks assured him.

Eubanks escorted Davy the rest of the way to Nashville, where he caught the stagecoach to Washington. He caused a pretty big stir when he tried to camp out near the White House. Some of the more experienced Congressmen laughed at him behind his back, and as they got bolder they began to laugh in his face. Davy was fuming.

"Got to control my temper," he thought. "They's nothing but skunks and weasels, unworthy of my fists."

"Introduce a bill," suggested an older Congressman who had befriended him. "Show 'em you've got a brain in your head."

Davy considered various subjects and stayed up half the night scribbling his first Washington speech on pieces of paper that he couldn't read afterward. The next day, when he was finally recognized, he got to his feet and stuttered a bit. Then he thought of something to say.

"In the time before time," he began, "when He Who Is Sky took a fancy to She Who Is Woman—I mean, She Who Is Earth—"

Everybody was laughing, even people in the balcony. Davy struggled for a while, then he got all tangled up in the history of the Indians and couldn't prove they had been cheated. After an hour of insults and war whoops from other Congressmen, Davy ceremoniously removed his black coat and rolled up his shirtsleeves.

"Would any of the gentlemen care to step outside and debate this matter further?" he asked, mocking their formal ways. But the Congressmen were frightened of him now and they avoided all discussion of his ideas. Davy went home to Tennessee a few months later, fed up with politics, still looking for a good fight.

Joe Magarac, Man of Steel

Steve Mestrovitch worked in an old, worn-out factory near Pittsburgh, Pennsylvania. His job was to shovel hunks of scrap metal into a big, red-hot furnace, where it would melt together with iron ore and limestone to make steel. Steve had been doing the same back-breaking job for thirty years, ever since he arrived from Hungary without knowing a word of English. Several of the younger men kidded him about getting old, but he could still lift more than his own weight with one hand, and he measured other men by their strength. He figured that if they were really strong they must also be honest and hardworking, like him and his friends.

Steve had been thinking about the younger men lately, because he was worried. His factory wasn't doing much business, and he might lose his job. Before that happened, he wanted to find a husband for his daughter, Mary, who was ready to start a family of her own. Mary liked educated men, of course, but Steve didn't trust them—he wanted his future son-in-law to be strong, dependable, and humble, like himself.

So Steve decided to organize a weight-lifting contest at the company picnic on July 4, 1903—maybe the last one they would ever have. He and his older friends arranged three stacks of steel bars under a chestnut tree: 350-pound bars that almost any man there could lift, 500 pounders in the middle, and 1,000-pound bars at the far end. If more than one young guy could lift that much, Steve would challenge them to try combinations.

"I'm warning you, Papa," said Mary. "I'm not going to marry some muscle-head

 just to please you. If I can't find a man with brains and a heart, I'll move into Pittsburgh and teach school."

When it was time for the weight-lifting contest, however, Mary was curious. She put on her Sunday dress and a wide-brimmed hat, and strolled down to the picnic grounds with two of her girlfriends.

The contest started. One by one the young men removed their ties and shirts, and each hoisted a 350-pound bar. Ten of them were able to lift 500 pounds over their heads. Three could lift 1,000 pounds. Then Steve Mestrovitch made them combine the weights. Two briefly lifted 1,350 pounds of steel, but neither could budge the next combination of 1,500 pounds.

Suddenly another man pushed through the crowd and asked if he could try.

"Sure, but who are you?" asked Steve.

"Joe Magarac, from Hungary," was the answer. "Come help you working mans. I man of steel."

People laughed, but they shut up quickly when Joe lifted two of the 1,000-pound steel bars together in his right hand, and looked around at the crowd.

"How you like?" said Joe.

Then he bent his knees and picked up two more 1,000-pound bars in his left hand, while holding the other two steady in his right.

"Four thousand pound," Joe said. "Enough? I win?"

Mary Mestrovich felt confused, almost dizzy—would this strange man just pick her up and carry her off? Her father was grinning from ear to ear as though he liked the idea. Joe Magarac spoke to him then, and the crowd hushed to listen.

"I win contest," he told Steve. "I no win daughter. She pick what man she want."

Mary and her father exchanged glances without saying anything. Joe Magarac climbed onto a picnic table and unbuttoned his faded blue shirt.

"See me now," he said. "I man of steel." His broad chest, his huge arms, his neck, his wrists, all seemed to be made of the purest shining metal. "Tomorrow I come work with you. We make good steel. More better than Carnegie. Better than anyones. You, me, we make most better steel in whole world."

Monday morning at six o'clock, Joe Magarac led the other men into the factory. Nobody hired him—he simply took over the largest furnace and showed them how to make the cleanest, straightest steel rails they had ever seen.

"Those for trains," said Joe. "Next we do big steel plates for building ships."

Everybody learned from Joe, and the factory became successful again. Steve kept his job. Mary married a schoolteacher. Snow came early. Just before Christmas, Joe Magarac was ready to move on.

"I go now," he told the workers. "You mans of steel."

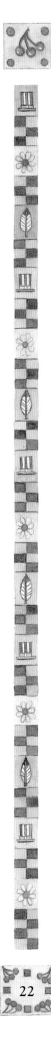

Paul Bunyan and His Blue Ox "Babe"

Shortly after her graduation from Radcliffe College, in 1910, Winifred Winslow learned that an elderly aunt had died and left her a lumber camp near Green Bay, Wisconsin. It came complete with several buildings, a sawmill, a crew of six, and a pile of unopened mail. Mostly bills, Winifred discovered, but a few checks as well, and a letter offering to purchase the whole business for one hundred thousand dollars.

"Take the money and run," Winifred's father advised her, glancing up from his *Boston Evening Transcript*. "Buy yourself some new clothes, find a husband, settle down."

Winifred ignored her father's advice, as usual. She bought some sensible shoes and trousers, said good-bye to a young man she had been seeing, and started out on her fateful journey to Green Bay, changing trains at Chicago and again at Milwaukee.

The lumber camp looked like a disaster when she arrived—buildings falling down, sawmill throwing dust and chips in all directions, logs scattered around haphazardly. But Winifred soon found that the lumbermen—"jacks" they called themselves—worked hard and generally knew what they were doing. All they needed was a little more direction and discipline, which she would be happy to provide.

When her parents visited Green Bay a year later, Winifred proudly showed them the tidy camp, the new roof on the bunkhouse, the men in their clean clothes coming and going, the neat stacks of timber. Her father had brought some mail from Boston, including a new offer of three hundred thousand dollars for Winifred's lumber company.

"Upping the ante," her father said. "Sell now, and make a nice profit. Start a dressmaking business or some such thing, if you like."

Winifred rejected the offer. Two weeks later, her crew of six lumberjacks quit to take better jobs at another logging camp across the bay. Just as Winifred was thinking of quitting too, a huge bearded man appeared in the doorway of her office.

"Name of Paul Bunyan," he said. "Heard you need help. I'll do the work of fifty lumberjacks for the wages of five."

"Indeed, Mr. Bunyan?" said Winifred, in a voice very much like her father's. "That's quite a tall order. Suppose we say you'll do the work of twenty men to start, for the wages of two."

"I don't know if I can work so little," said Paul Bunyan. "It's a fraction of what I'm used to. But I'll try."

Winifred watched him at first, but he moved so fast and so far that she soon gave up. He could chop down a hundred trees an hour, have them trimmed and stacked next to the sawmill in twenty minutes, then cut them into twelve-foot lengths, faster than her mother's Irish cook could cut up string beans.

"But how can you move all this wood down to the lake and make rafts out of it?" Winifred asked him.

"No problem," said Paul Bunyan. "Babe will help, soon as she gets back from vacation."

Winifred expected a female version of Paul Bunyan himself, muscular and hairy, but Babe turned out to be a gigantic blue ox.

"And she's blue because . . . ?" Winifred asked.

"'Cause she was born in the sky over Lake Michigan," Paul Bunyan replied. "That's where she goes every year on vacation. Up among the stars."

He fastened all the lengths of wood he had cut into one great bundle, tied with roots and saplings. Then Babe started hauling it toward the lake, knocking live trees out of the way, gouging a trench some ten feet deep and thirty feet wide.

"Next time we just flood that trench," said Paul Bunyan. "Float the logs down."

"And what will Babe do next?" Winifred asked.

"She wants to try running the sawmill."

Winifred sat in her office, while Babe did a day's work in the blink of an eye—twelve-foot logs flew out of the sawmill like bullets from a machine gun.

Feeling strangely discouraged, almost depressed, Winifred sent a Western Union telegram to her father. She told him that running the lumber camp was getting too easy for her, and he telegraphed his reply immediately.

"Know what you mean. Success comes too easily to most of us Winslows. Sell for half a million. Come home. Try something more challenging, like the Harvard Law School."

Winifred was pleased for once to take her father's good advice.

Pecos Bill Rides a Mountain Lion

Bill Kimble found work on a ranch near the Rio Grande River, back in the days when Texas was young and big and tough, like Bill himself. His boss gave him the job of hauling water from the river to fill shallow clay basins where thirsty cattle could drink. There were dozens of these basins scattered across the ranch, and Bill labored from sunup to sundown to keep them full. At first he used wooden buckets, carrying six in each hand, but he spilled too much water that way. His boss showed him a stack of empty barrels in the barn and an old wagon.

"You'll have to pull it yourself," the boss said. "I don't have horses to spare."

Bill was scared of his boss, a mean little fellow who looked like a cactus with a mustache, so he didn't argue. From week to week, however, he noticed that the level of water in the Rio Grande was lower and lower. It got harder and harder for him to fill his barrels, even out in the middle of the river, and finally he had to tell his boss the bad news.

"Well, you're just going to have to find water somewhere else," his boss replied, "if you want to keep on working here."

Bill went running that night, and made a big circle around the ranch, looking for ponds or streams that might keep the cattle going until this dry spell was over. Even the smallest water holes were empty. At dawn he searched the sky for signs of rain, but there wasn't a cloud in sight.

"What about the Pecos River?" his boss asked.

"Dry as a bone," said Bill.

"I heard there was water in it further up," the boss insisted. "Take another look."

Bill finished breakfast and followed the dry, narrow bed of the river northward. After a few miles he discovered some shallow puddles of water—not enough to fill many barrels, but better than nothing. A passing cowboy told him there was a lake in the hills beyond. Bill hurried back to the ranch and asked his boss if he could borrow a plow.

"I'll cut a channel up to the lake," Bill explained, "but first I'll dig us a pond at this end, so the water won't just run away when it gets here."

Bill took off his shirt and boots and started pushing the plow around the soft, sandy soil. It was easy work for him and by suppertime he had made a hole half a mile across and forty feet deep.

"Not bad," his boss admitted, "but it still don't have no water in it."

Early the next morning, Bill cut an opening in the north side of the pond and pushed his plow swiftly up the dry riverbed toward the lake he'd heard about. Mile

 after mile, through sand or gravel, he straightened and deepened the channel. When he reached the lake, however, it was almost empty, and the hoofprints of cattle around the edge told him it must be heavily used.

"Got to go further," Bill thought.

As the moon rose he left the lake behind, pushing steadily northward with his plow. He came to an old wagon trail, where a faded sign pointed left toward Fort Stockton, and he kept going. By noon the next day he crossed the border into New Mexico, but there still wasn't enough water in the Pecos River to wet more than his bare feet. Somewhere in the hills between Santa Fe and Las Vegas, he found a bubbling spring where the river actually began, and there was nothing more to plow.

That afternoon Bill sat beside his river, watching a shiny trickle of water start its journey southward, wondering what to do next. He fell asleep. Gradually the sky darkened, and rain came pouring down, filling the river, overflowing, soaking the dry land. Bill woke up and laughed triumphantly. He had succeeded!

"But I'm not going back to Texas," he realized. "I been there, I done that."

Reaching into a nearby cave, Bill pulled out a reluctant rattlesnake, made a loop of it, and roped a wet, bewildered mountain lion to ride on. Snake and lion soon understood who was boss. When the rain stopped, Bill dried himself with tumbleweed and moved out, eager for the adventures he knew he would find in the country west of the Pecos.

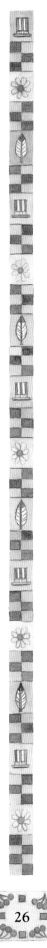

Kilroy Was Here

Near the end of World War II, an American soldier named Joe Donahue came home to South Bend, Indiana. He was so tired he wanted to sleep for a week, but he proudly carried a duffel bag full of souvenirs—helmets, flags, medals, and insignias from four different armies, among other things.

Joe's greatest treasure, carefully wrapped in his one clean shirt, was a smooth piece of dark metal with the words *"Kilroy was here"* written in chalk. He put it on the shelf in the living-room, between his bowling trophies, and wouldn't let anyone else touch it.

"What is it?" his children asked.

"Part of a German tank," he told them.

"What does it mean?" asked his wife.

Joe explained that he had found this thing among the ruins of an Italian village, after a tough battle.

"I was the first GI to enter that town," he said. "At least I thought I was. The whole place was full of smoke, and some of the houses were on fire. I ran from doorway to doorway, afraid of snipers. But the town was empty. Down the street, I saw this big Tiger tank stuck between two buildings. The hatch on the turret was wide open. I climbed up to have a look. Inside, I found 'Kilroy' written on this steel panel beside the radio. So I unscrewed it and took it with me."

"But what does it mean?" his wife persisted.

"It means some other GI was the first one into that town. Into that tank. I thought I was, but I wasn't—do you see what I mean? I can't understand how anybody could have gotten in there ahead of me, but somebody did."

"Maybe some German wrote it. Or some Italian."

"No, this was strictly U.S. Whoever got anywhere first—any-hard-to-get-to place, I mean—they would write this for other guys to find."

"But who was Kilroy?" Joe's children asked.

"Just a name, I guess," said Joe. "It could just as well be Smith or Jones—or Dwight D. Eisenhower, for that matter."

Thirty years later, in 1975, Joe Donahue went to a reunion of war veterans in Chicago, and got to talking with some of his old buddies about Kilroy.

"I heard it was all a fake," said one veteran. "There was no such person."

"No," said another. "There was a real guy, but he didn't use his right name."

"Couldn't have been just one guy, or half a dozen guys," said Joe. "They had to be in too many different places at once."

"So who was Kilroy?"

"I'll tell you," said a quiet man with a scarred face. "I happened to hear the story from a cousin of mine, who grew up near Quincy, Mass."

The other veterans gathered around, and the quiet man continued.

"There really was a guy named Kilroy, James J. Kilroy, who worked at the naval shipyard in Quincy during the war, building destroyers. His younger brother, Paul, a sailor, had been killed on a freighter that was torpedoed out in the North Atlantic. After that, Kilroy did everything he could to get into the war, but he had flat feet and bad eyesight, so they wouldn't take him. Then he decided that making ships would be his way of fighting back. And he put his name on each one he worked on. I mean, he couldn't do it officially, or put it where too many people would see it right away. So just before a ship was launched, he would crawl way up inside the bow, or maybe climb the mast, or something like that, and write '*Kilroy was here.*' And sooner or later somebody would find it and the idea would spread."

"I saw it in Korea," a veteran said.

"My nephew saw it in Vietnam," another said.

"So there you are," said Joe. "It wasn't just a guy, it was a whole lot of guys, trying to give each other a laugh."

"But whatever happened to James J. Kilroy?" a veteran asked.

"Why don't you call him up and find out?" one of the others replied. "If he's for real, maybe he's still listed in the telephone directory in Quincy, Mass."

The veteran went looking for a phone booth. A few minutes later he returned to his expectant friends.

"I got the number, and dialed it, and somebody answered," he reported, "but Kilroy wasn't there."

Uncle Sam

Samuel Wilson was nobody's hero—not even his own. Although he worked for a small company that supplied meat to the United States Army during the 1840s, he never got within two thousand miles of any fighting. Sam was a patriotic young man, however, and when the war with Mexico erupted, he felt he had to help. So he started writing brief messages on the smooth wooden barrels of salted pork and beef as he packed them for shipment.

"*Greetings to U.S. soldiers,*" he'd say, using heavy black crayon, "*from yr. loyal friend Sam'l. Wilson of Troy, New York.*"

After repeating this wording dozens of times he decided to have a little fun with it, so he signed himself "*yr. loving uncle Sam Wilson,*" even though he wasn't much older than most of the troops.

One day Sam received a wrinkled letter that had come all the way from a military post office at Galveston, Texas.

"Dear Uncle Sam," the letter said. "We may not make it home from this blamed neck of the woods, but here's eight of us got no other relatives on the face of the earth, so to you Uncle we say 'Thankee' for good food & kind words." Six signatures followed, plus two Xs, and then a P.S. "We're wondering what do you look like?"

Sam looked like many other young men—brown hair, medium height, slightly on the heavy side of average. He assumed the soldiers would prefer a more interesting Uncle than that, however, so he wandered around town on the Fourth of July, studying the flags and decorations, listening to people talk. After much thought he came up with the following description.

"I'm a lean and sinewy old man," he wrote, *"with long white hair and white chin whiskers, eyes of fiercest blue, and a nose like the prow of a fighting ship. This year I'm wearing a tall blue hat with stars spangled on it. My pantaloons are in stripes of red and white, and my blue swallowtail coat has stars on it, too. I love these United States more dearly than the bald eagle loves his chicks. I've got fists like rocks but fingers that can play a fiddle better than the best music-makers of Europe. Friends say I'm as ferocious as a grizzly bear, yet cool as a cucumber. Though I may be gentle with those weaker than myself, I can honestly swear that I've never run from a battle nor lost a fight."*

As a matter of fact, young Sam Wilson had never won a fight, either, and he hadn't been in a battle anywhere, but he saw no point in saying so. He added a few more paragraphs of fanciful details and mailed this letter off to his eight homesick "nephews" near the Mexican border.

Several weeks later he happened to see a newspaper from Albany, New York, with a headline that pulled him up short.

"UNCLE SAM VISITS TROOPS IN TEXAS," it said. Underneath was a drawing very much like the character he had described in his letter, and a long story about Uncle Sam cheering up the American soldiers.

"He strode among us like a giant among midgets," an excited young corporal from Rhode Island was quoted as saying, "and in his footprints a thousand American banners sprang up like red, white, and blue flowers." Other soldiers made similar statements, full of wild enthusiasm. As he read these words, Sam Wilson feared that his creation, Uncle Sam, was getting out of hand. What should he do about it?

"For one thing, I'll quit writing messages on the meat barrels," he decided. "Nothing but plain old 'U.S. Army' from now on."

But he saw more newspaper stories about Uncle Sam as time went by, and he began to realize that, wherever this thing might be going, he couldn't stop it now. Even after the Mexican War ended, Uncle Sam kept popping up in other places, both at home and abroad, and when the Civil War broke out in 1861, Uncle Sam appeared to be supporting both sides. Confederate soldiers talked and wrote letters about him, while Yankee soldiers were claiming him for their own.

Year after year, so many new "nephews" and "nieces" responded to his colorful creation that Samuel Wilson felt no need to raise a family. He often visited the homes of his younger brothers and sisters, though, and he loved it when their children addressed him as "Uncle Sam."

The River God's Wife

Li Liang lived in a community of Chinese Americans near the Sacramento River in California. He had worked hard as a vegetable grower for more than forty years, and his back was permanently bent, but now that he had retired from farming he wanted to see a little further than before. So each morning, after drinking his tea, Li Liang would climb slowly to the top of the earth-  en levee which separated the river from the wide green fields, and look eagerly upstream and down. He'd gaze with pride upon a barge carrying crops to San Francisco and the world beyond, or a freighter bringing goods from afar to his beloved Delta country. He'd wave excitedly at power boats as they roared along, full of young people who seldom waved back. But his favorites were the sailboats, graceful as swans, tacking gradually up the river or gliding smoothly downstream. Sometimes they'd pass so close that Li Liang could see the occupants clearly—and if there happened to be a beautiful girl among them, he would clap his calloused hands with true delight.

"That one would make a good wife for the River God," he'd murmur to himself.

Nobody ever heard him say this, or wondered what he meant, until his oldest daughter accompanied him to the top of the levee one morning. Her name was Agnes Liang, but people called her "The Hag" behind her back, because she was big, ugly, and shockingly disrespectful to her widowed father, for whom she kept house.

"So what's the special attraction, Old Man?" she barked. "You drag your pitiful carcass up here to see what, exactly?"

Li Liang ignored her, as he usually did. Agnes glared at the river. For some time it remained empty, as if it were frightened by her loud and threatening voice. Then a boat appeared around the bend, motoring, with sails hanging loose. Two people stood on the bow, a male and a female, wearing bathing suits.

Staring at them as the boat drew closer, Li Liang murmured appreciatively. The female was blonde, no longer young, but she seemed to gather the light of the river into her glowing skin and her pale hair. Splendid! Adorable! Li Liang grabbed his daughter's arm without thinking, and pointed towards the boat.

"That one would make a good wife for the River God!" he exclaimed.

Agnes twisted out of her father's grip, and stepped away from him angrily. *River God?* This river was flat, muddy, as ugly as she was herself. She glanced down again at the man on the sailboat. *River God?* Ridiculous! Then she remembered her father telling a story when she was very young—when her mother was still alive, and all three of them were happy together.

After the sailboat had vanished around the next bend of the river, Agnes returned to her father's side, and spoke to him in a gentler voice.

"Tell me the story of the River God, please," she said, as though she were a child again. Her father smiled at her.

"Long ago," he began, "when our ancestors lived near China's greatest river, some wicked officials would come to them in the spring and kidnap the most beautiful young females, using the excuse that a suitable wife must be found for the River God. Some of these girls were later returned to their families in exchange for money, but most of them were never seen again. All except one, the most splendid and adorable each year—this young beauty would be hurled pleading and screaming into the rushing waters of the Yangtze Gorge."

"So what happened?" Agnes asked.

"So a handsome stranger arrived by boat, a hero larger than life, just as an incredibly lovely young woman was about to be sacrificed. He was instantly smitten with love for her, and she for him. However, he hid his true feelings and pretended he was furious with the wicked officials for choosing someone not worthy of being the River God's wife! One by one he threw those greedy men into the river, until the rest ran away and the people of the province cheered."

Li Liang fell silent, lost in his thoughts. Agnes studied the river and the passing boats with new interest. She accompanied her father to the levee every morning after that, and her ugly face gradually softened as she opened herself up to the beauty of the world around her. She might never become splendid and adorable like the River God's wife, of course, but the neighbors began to notice how different she looked when they saw her in a certain light.

Pocahontas

Amerca's first love story begins like a fairy tale. *Once upon a time, there was a handsome prince who fell in love with a beautiful princess, and rescued her from—*no, that's not it.

Once upon a time there was a beautiful princess, who fell in love with a handsome man and rescued him from being killed by her father's guards. The princess was called Pocahontas, the man was a stranger, and the story took place in the lush green wilderness of Virginia, as it looked to early settlers from England.

John Smith, who played the part of the prince in this story, was considered an adventurer in real life, or maybe an opportunist. Energetic, dashing, bold, Captain Smith made few lasting friends. He traveled frequently, yet he wasn't fully satisfied by the places he had visited, such as Turkey or the Ukraine. Deep inside he felt that newer, more exciting places were awaiting him, somewhere beyond the horizon. So he turned his attention away from Europe, and sailed across the ocean to America with a group of men and women who hoped to establish themselves as farmers in the colonies claimed by England. They reached the Virginia coast in 1607, and named their new settlement "Jamestown" to honor James the First, their King.

It was not a happy landing. Some of these eager newcomers might have been successful at farming back home, where the plow slid easily through the rich soil, but they lacked the knowledge and the tools needed to start from scratch. Here they found dense forests growing to the water's edge, and swamps that seemed bottomless. Weather was either uncomfortably cold and damp or miserably hot and humid. Flies and mosquitoes pestered them. Wild animals attacked. After dark, they listened to growling and howling and other terrifying noises. Who could tell what hideous monsters might be lurking in the trees? What heartless savages might be preparing to strike?

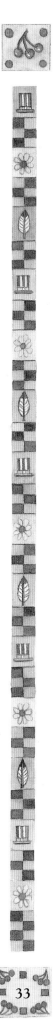

The truth is that most of the wild animals wanted nothing to do with these people, but their environment had been disturbed, so they made noises about it. Bears growled, wolves howled, birds squawked, and wild dogs barked nervously at any sound.

Among the so-called savages—that is, the Native Americans who were already living in Virginia—there were mixed reactions to the arrival and settlement of strangers, one shipload after another. Some natives regarded the European settlers as enemies to be driven away. Others saw them as evil demons to be killed. And a few, including Princess Pocahontas, were fascinated by the sight of these foreign people, many of them blond and pale-skinned, in their black and white clothes. It was as though gods and goddesses had landed, or beings from the moon—the thrill of a lifetime!

Captain Smith stood out from the other English colonists. Bigger, bolder, and more colorful, he did not enjoy sharing their dull lives. By night he kept watch with some of them, talking about farming and fishing, while secretly hoping for excitement. By day he ventured into the woods alone, sword in hand, seeking he wasn't sure what.

One afternoon, several miles from the settlement, Smith was captured and disarmed by two men who looked as strange to him as he did to them. Almost naked, dark-skinned, their faces painted to inspire fear, the men tied Smith with leather thongs and led him through the woods to a hidden village. It consisted of wooden huts built around a clearing, with a larger ceremonial building at one end. Inside, the Chieftain or King sat on a brightly decorated throne, with most of the tribe in attendance. Smith, still tied up, had to lie on the dirt floor while everyone regarded him silently. Presently the King, whose name was Powhatan, gave a signal, and pointed to the center of the space, where two massive stones formed a platform.

What happened next was described by Smith himself in a book he completed years later. Several of King Powhatan's guards dragged him across the dirt floor and forced him to kneel with his head on one of the stones. They were "ready with their clubs, to beat out his brains," he wrote, when a loud and melodramatic voice interrupted them.

"Stop! Father, I beg of you, tell them to stop!"

The crowd gasped and drew back, as Powhatan's daughter, Pocahontas, dashed forward, pleading with her father to have mercy. The guards, fearful of her anger, hes-

itated to strike at Smith. But the King impatiently ordered them to go ahead. As people shouted and screamed, Pocahontas threw herself across Smith's body, resting her head on his head.

"Kill me instead," she cried.

This her father would not do, of course, and everyone waited to see what would happen next. The crowd of onlookers whispered among themselves while Pocahontas sobbed. Smith, bearing her weight on his body, his face wet from her tears, could only guess at what these people were saying. He was torn between discomfort and relief, and something more—never in his fantasies of high adventure had he imagined a scene of such drama and romance, and here it was actually happening!

The King usually granted his favorite child anything she asked for, and usually she got bored before long. So, Powhatan thought, if Pocahontas wanted to amuse herself with this foreigner, this pathetic figure dressed in dusty black like a molting crow—why not? She'd soon tire of the fellow. Therefore Powhatan gave an order, servants helped the Princess to her feet, and Captain Smith was quickly untied.

Standing before the King, Pocahontas and Smith looked at each other with the most intense curiosity. He was struck by her vivid beauty, her regal bearing, the passionate interest in her eyes. She smiled, sensing the

adventurous heart that beat within him, much like her own. Thoughts and feelings passed between them like a new language. *Freedom! Discovery! Love! Or something like love, at least for this moment.*

Together they left the King's presence and wandered into the forest. With no effort they soon learned to communicate, partly in the language of her people, partly in English. Smith offered her a piece of ginger candy from his pocket, and she chewed it greedily.

Pocahontas was hardly more than a child, he gradually realized, in spite of her stunning appearance, and Smith himself was not the ladies' man he sometimes pretended to be. So when this young Princess spoke glowingly but vaguely on the subject of adult intimacy—about which she knew almost nothing—Smith didn't want to disillusion her. For him, Pocahontas was not so much a real person as an image of natural beauty. For her, the dashing Captain was not meant to be a suitor but someone sent to guide her away from where she lived, into a different world.

Under the watchful eyes of King Powhatan's guards, the Princess and the Captain met often in the woods. They walked, they talked, and during the next two years they educated each other. Smith told Pocahontas stories about life in England, and some of his exciting experiences in other countries as well, a fascinating mixture of fact and fiction. She taught him the myths of her people, the legends and prayers, and as much as she knew about the lands traditionally occupied by her father's tribe. As he absorbed this information, Smith was already imagining himself "discovering" more of America before other Europeans could get to it.

After receiving a fond farewell from the blossoming young Princess and what seemed to be a generous gift of territory from her father—who was glad to get rid of him—Smith sailed north from Jamestown in 1609. He carefully explored the Chesapeake Bay and other coastal areas, which he had reason to believe were now his, and drew maps. Continuing northward, Smith took his ship into many of the major rivers and harbors of "New England," which he named and mapped years before the Pilgrims landed there in 1620. Somewhere in the course of his northern voyages he began to call himself "Admiral" Smith, rather than "Captain," as he sought credit for these discoveries. He did not return to Virginia.

Pocahontas was only seventeen when John Smith sailed out of her life. She missed him greatly for a while, but then she fell in love and married another English settler, John Rolfe, who promised to take her to London. Several years later he happily did so. Pocahontas, accompanied by ten of her father's Indian guards, caused a sensation in the English capital. Everyone wanted to meet her and every door was open to her, from palaces to taverns. Before long she became ill with smallpox, and despite the best efforts of the Queen's physicians, she died in her husband's arms at age twenty-one.

George Washington and the Cherry Tree

George Washington was born on a small plantation in the English colony of Virginia, not far from the point where the long and unhurried Potomac River, twisting back and forth, finally meets the waters of the Chesapeake Bay. This is called "tidewater" country, because it is close to the Atlantic Ocean. It is still inhabited by good-hearted people who live on farms, plant crops, fish, raise families, mind their own business, and use boats and horses when they go to visit friends.

One day in 1735, when George was three years old, the family came sailing back from just such a visit to find that their modest home had burned to the ground. All of their belongings were destroyed, and the cause of the fire was unknown. George's mother thought that they should rebuild the house and start over, but his father had other ideas. After giving some instructions to the workers who remained behind, he helped his wife and children back into their boat and took them more than a hundred miles up the Potomac to a larger plantation that he also owned. There he had a new house built. Small at first, it grew as Washington's family grew, and it came to be the mansion we know today as Mount Vernon.

When George was a little boy, however, none of that future comfort and elegance could be imagined. Home had only two bedrooms at first, one for parents and the other for children, a big all-purpose room downstairs, no formal dining room or par-

lor. Only sheds for cooking and other necessities. Not a hint of the white columns, the wide verandah where George and his wife would sit and rock in later years, looking down towards the river and the woods beyond. Instead of roads and parkways, nothing but footpaths and a rough trail meandering through fields and forest in the general direction of Alexandria and what is now the city of Washington.

As simple as it was, young George enjoyed his new home more than he had the earlier one. His older brothers went off to school, but he had visiting cousins to play with, chickens to chase around the farmyard, trees to climb, the river for swimming, fishing, and crabbing. The farm itself was busy with things to see and do, though George was not yet big enough to help very much. There was also a blacksmith's shop and a joinery, where furniture and tools were produced. Sometimes toys for the younger children. George played with wooden soldiers, a painted wagon that had horses to pull it, and a very clever gadget that made a hand-carved monkey leap up and turn somersaults when two handles were squeezed together.

He was a smart little boy, educated at home by relatives and tutors, and as he got to be five years old, the pleasures of childhood were beginning to bore him. George observed his older brothers coming and going freely, on horses of their own, while he usually stayed at home. They were allowed to use tools, knives, even guns, while he had to be content with pieces of wood. After dinner on his fifth birthday, George asked Augustine Washington, his father, for permission to carry a sword. The response was delighted laughter.

"A sword? You dearest, most extraordinary fellow, what will you be thinking of next?"

"But I mean to be a soldier one day, Father, and I must begin preparing myself as soon as possible."

"My darling boy," his father answered kindly, "you are much too young for such things as swords, and I pray you may never have need to use them."

"But, Father—"

"No, George, a sword is out of the question. Perhaps you can amuse yourself with this gift from your grandmother."

Mr. Washington reached into the side pocket of his long coat and presented George with a slender object wrapped in blue paper. Opening it, the boy discovered a pocket knife with one long blade and a smooth ivory handle.

"Father, thank you, thank you!"

"Happy birthday, my dear son."

During the following year, this little knife became George's sword, his tomahawk, his wood chisel, and many other things in games he played. He would treasure it for the rest of his life—but he soon realized that he couldn't cut very much with it. Again he went to Augustine Washington for permission.

"I need a saw, Father, or an axe, so that I can help the men clearing brush from the new pasture."

"Very well," Mr. Washington replied, after some thought. "I will consider having an axe or a saw made for you, when you are six. But you must promise me," he continued, as George hugged him in gratitude, "you must promise me, my son, that whatever I give you, it will never be used in harmful or destructive ways."

"Of course I promise, Father," George said, his thoughts racing ahead. "And must I really wait all those months until my next birthday?"

"I will think about it and discuss it with your mother," Augustine Washington assured him.

Not long after that, George and his father watched the blacksmith finishing a shiny little hatchet, which immediately took the place of his pocket knife in the boy's daily activities. But now there was a difference. Instead of playing, he helped with the actual work of the household—chopping sticks for kindling wood, trimming some evergreen branches to decorate the new dining room.

At breakfast in that very room, several weeks later, George's father made a stunning announcement. He was planning to turn this farm over to a nephew, now that it was established and prosperous. The family would move somewhere else.

"Fruit trees will be planted here, along with corn and hay, and I expect them to flourish," Mr. Washington explained.

George felt his personal world falling apart, and he withdrew silently to a secret place in the woods nearby, where he wept. The next day he felt better, and as time passed with no more talk of moving, he began to hope that his father's plans might have changed yet again.

On a crisp morning in March, however, George saw an English ship tied up to the dock below the farm. Men were unloading dozens of young fruit trees, roots wrapped in burlap, and pulling them up the hill in handcarts. During the next two days, several of the fields closest to the house were transformed into orchards. Soon Mr. Washington's nephew would be arriving to take charge, and the family would move away from here—perhaps forever.

George felt depressed, then angry about the disruption of his young life. Not just angry—furious! As soon as the planting was completed, and the workmen had left, he rushed outdoors to look at the new trees: apple and cherry, pear and peach, plum and something else he didn't recognize. Such young, perfect, innocent trees, brought all the way from England at great expense—and now George hated them.

Seizing his hatchet, which he often wore in a loop of leather hanging from his belt, George ran angrily through the new orchards, swiping left and right at branches, buds, and blossoms. He left a trail of pink and white petals behind him. But it was not enough to injure these new enemies—he wanted to *destroy* them! Thwack! He started chopping at the trunk of a cherry tree close to the house. Thwack, thwack! His hatchet cut deeper. Chips flew. Soon the young tree was leaning over. Thwack, thwack, thwack! Finally with a satisfying crack and a sigh, the cherry tree fell to the ground.

About to attack another tree, George suddenly caught himself and stopped, as though his father was there to restrain him. He still felt upset, angry, but now he felt remorse as well—the tree had done him no harm, after all, and his parents had taught

him to respect all living things. And his father! What would George's father think, when he was told this terrible news?

All that afternoon, George waited by the gate for Augustine Washington to come riding home from Alexandria. As dusk fell, he saw the beloved figure of his parent approaching.

"Father, Father!" he cried. "The most dreadful thing has happened to one of our new trees—there, by the house!"

Augustine Washington quickly dismounted, examined the damage to the cherry tree, and picked up George in his arms.

"Whoever did this, George?" he asked.

"I did, Father," the boy said, bursting into tears. "I did, I did it—I cannot lie to you."

George wanted to explain why he had cut down the tree, he wanted to say how sorry he was, but his father interrupted.

"Later, my dearest boy, later I'll want to know all about it. At this moment, George, the most important thing, the only really important thing, is that you have told me the truth!"

Riding high in his father's arms, young George Washington felt like a conquering hero.

Honest Abe

When he was twenty-five years old, Abraham Lincoln decided to run for a seat in the state legislature. He didn't look like a politician—homely, uncomfortably tall, wearing faded old clothes, awkward as a giraffe on the move. And his previous experience didn't add up to much—farming, odd jobs, a year's service as village postmaster. But he had educated himself by reading books and asking questions, and he sincerely wanted to serve the people of his district. He knew a lot of them already. Now he was going to meet others, walking from one farm to the next along the dusty back roads of rural Illinois.

Early one evening, Lincoln stopped near a split-rail fence to wipe his sweaty face and rest for a moment. In the field beyond, a farmer was cutting hay in rows, the old-fashioned way, swinging a long-handled blade called a scythe. As Lincoln watched, the man finished a row and then came towards him, carrying the scythe. He was a healthy-looking young fellow, about Lincoln's age, and he seemed friendly enough.

"Looking for someone?" he asked. "I'm Frank Chapin."

Lincoln introduced himself, and Frank laughed pleasantly.

"I've heard about you already," he said. "Some people call you 'Honest Abe.' But why in the world would an honest man want to be in politics?"

Lincoln laughed too.

"Frank, let me tell you why *I* want to be in politics," he replied.

Before Lincoln could explain what he hoped to accomplish, he was interrupted by a bell ringing at the farmhouse on the hill.

"That's my wife calling me to dinner," said Frank. "Why don't you come along, Abe, and eat with us? I'd like to hear more about your ideas."

Lincoln knew a meal awaited him at home, so he declined politely.

"I'll tell you what, though," he added. "If you'll let me use the scythe while you're eating dinner, I'll cut a couple of rows of hay for you."

"Why, thank you, Abe."

Frank handed him the scythe, together with the whetstone that was used to sharpen it every so often, and hurried up the hill. While eating dinner he told his wife, Peggy, about Abraham Lincoln.

"Sounds too good to be true," she commented.

When Frank returned to the field, he found three rows of hay neatly cut. Lincoln was gone. The scythe leaned against a tall gate-post, but where was the whetstone? Frank couldn't find it anywhere.

"Why in the world would an honest man want to steal a thing like that?" he asked his wife.

"I'm not surprised," Peggy replied. "I told you nobody could be as honest as they say he is."

"It's only worth half a dollar," Frank said. But he felt disappointed. This wasn't just a matter of money.

Almost thirty years later, when Lincoln was President of the United States, the Chapins went to a White House reception with other voters from Illinois. There were city people and lawyers and small-town folks and soldiers and farmers in the line waiting to meet the President. Frank and Peggy didn't expect more than a handshake and a brief word or two, but as they approached Lincoln he smiled warmly and greeted Frank by name.

"You actually remember my husband after all these years?" Peggy asked.

"Indeed I do," the President replied, and he described their earlier meeting in some detail.

"That's amazing," Frank said. "But I have to ask you a question, Mr. President. Why in the world did you take my whetstone?"

Lincoln thought for a moment, then his homely face lighted up.

"I remember," he said. "I left your scythe leaning against a gate-post, and I put the whetstone up on top."

When the Chapins got back to their farm, they stopped at the gate, and Frank stood up in the wagon so that he could see the top of the seven-foot post.

"It's here," he told Peggy.

"I'm not surprised," said she. "Nobody as smart as Abe Lincoln would lie about a thing like that."

Theodore Roosevelt and the Teddy Bear

Theodore Roosevelt, President of the United States from 1901 to 1909, was an indoor man who spent as much time outdoors as he could. Short, near-sighted, looking more like a professor than a soldier or a sportsman, Roosevelt loved reading and writing, yet he embraced the world of action too. His favorite activities included hunting, fishing, swimming, riding horses, camping with his wife, and taking the children on hikes.

Sunday afternoons, for instance, the President could be seen walking from the White House to Rock Creek Park. He moved briskly, talking all the while. Family, friends, guests—whoever came along had to follow the leader in a straight line, not going *around* trees and boulders and other obstacles but climbing *over* them, up one side and down the other. Sometimes Roosevelt would lead the way into the Potomac River—aiming for a wooded island which is now kept in its natural state as a memorial to him. One after another, children and grownups waded or swam across, to find towels and picnic baskets awaiting them under canvas shelters.

When he was away from home, Roosevelt would write newsy letters to the children, describing his adventures and illustrating them with little sketches of birds, animals, or people that might be of interest. But there was one hunting story he didn't share with them at first. This was the episode of the "Teddy Bear," which added to his fame and popularity in a way that caused him some embarrassment.

In 1902, several of Roosevelt's friends invited him to join them on a hunting trip in Mississippi. They assured him that the black bears down there were as big and ferocious as the brown grizzlies he had encountered out West. Roosevelt said he doubted this, but he accepted the invitation and left Washington on a week's vacation. The trip was disappointing. Rainy weather, wet tents, ticks on the dogs, and no bears! By the end of the week, Roosevelt's friends were desperate. They sent the guides out all day looking for a bear, any bear. At last one was found, and the guides took the President towards it through the brush.

When they came to a clearing, everyone stopped. Tied to a tree with a rope around its neck was a small black bear, looking old, frightened, tired—or maybe sick.

"What's this?" asked the President.

The guides told him it was a bear they had captured for him to shoot. Otherwise his trip would be wasted.

"I'm sorry you went to all this trouble," Roosevelt said. He explained it wouldn't be possible for him to shoot an animal under these circumstances.

"We'll untie it," they said. "Then you can shoot it while it's moving."

"Just let it go," the President replied.

So the little old bear was released. It crawled back into the woods as rapidly as it could. Roosevelt returned to Washington the next day and said nothing to the public about his hunting trip. But one or two newspapers got the story, somehow, and the *Washington Post* published a drawing of the kindhearted President, rifle in hand, refusing to shoot that poor old bear. Other newspapers picked up the story. Soon people all over the country, all over the world, were talking about "Teddy's bear."

As the story spread, details were changed. The little old bear, tired or sick-looking, with black fur, became a *young* bear, cute and cuddly, with brown fur. Artists made drawings of the President's encounter with this fictitious creature. Roosevelt was shown gazing at it fondly, and it looked back with gratitude in its big brown eyes.

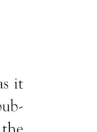

Thus the "Teddy Bear" was born. A small company in Brooklyn, New York, began to make Teddy Bear toys for sale in local stores. Bigger companies made them as well. Before long, Teddy Bears were being manufactured and sold everywhere. They are still popular toys—even among people who have no idea where the name "Teddy" actually came from.

When Roosevelt realized that his children would hear about it sooner or later, he told them his version of the story and waited anxiously for their response. Alice, the oldest, was unforgiving as usual.

"It's wrong to shoot helpless animals," she said sternly. "Even if you let one go occasionally, it's still not right to shoot the others."

But the other children believed that their beloved father could do no wrong, and Quentin, the youngest, wanted to know when he could have a Teddy Bear of his very own.

Other Tales of Characters Larger Than Life

Peter Francisco was only sixteen years old when the American Revolution broke out, in 1776, but he tried to join the army. Turned away because of his age, he ran across the battlefield, knocked aside some British soldiers, hitched himself to a cannon and pulled it back to the American lines. Using his enormous size and strength to do what seemed impossible, Peter performed dozens of other amazing feats during several years of service to his country.

Joe Call fought in the War of 1812 and became famous for wrestling any challenger, American or British, between battles. Later, when Joe was working peacefully as a farmer in Lewis County, New York, another celebrated strong man traveled all the way from London to take him on—but departed abruptly after he saw Joe lift a heavy iron plow with one hand and wave it in the air.

Big Frank earned his living as a migrant farm worker, following the wheat harvest from Texas to the Dakotas. He could do more work and do it faster than anybody else, until he got so hot that steam came out of his ears. Then he would dam up a creek or drain a pond to quench his thirst. Once he squeezed the juice out of a whole silo full of corn, drank his fill, and slept for a week.

Big Sixteen was a black man who got his name from the size of his shoes. He was huge, strong, and fearless, yet as gentle as an angel to others. When the Devil kept bothering his neighbors, Big Sixteen fought with the Devil and killed him, only to discover that the Devil had a fire-breathing wife and a pack of children who were very upset and eager to get revenge.

Annie Christmas, a black woman who gave generously to the poor in New Orleans, was six-feet-eight-inches tall and weighed 250 pounds. Living a rough and tumble life, Annie showed many a tough guy the way to go home, until she finally met a man who could beat her in a fight. She fell in love with him, much to her own surprise, but she didn't win his heart.

Diamond Jim Brady spent a lot of money on flashy jewelry and expensive meals. Having stuffed himself for years, he finally collapsed after eating one of his enormous dinners at a hotel in Baltimore. According to legend, Brady's life was saved by doctors who replaced his worn-out stomach with one taken from a recently deceased elephant. Brady sold his diamond cufflinks to pay the bill.

The Sky Woman, wife of the Chief of Heaven, was carried down to the endless waters of this world by birds that also helped to build an island for her to rest on. As the island became larger, plants and animals grew on it, and its beauty pleased the Sky

Woman so much that she asked if she could stay. The Chief of Heaven agreed, and she changed her name to the Great Earth Mother.

Amazons, women of fabulous power, inhabited the mysterious island of Feminea, somewhere in the Atlantic Ocean. They had little use for men, but sometimes they rescued the crews of fishing boats lost at sea and allowed them to visit briefly before sending them away. Later explorers looked for Feminea without success during their voyages to America, and eventually it ceased to be shown on the maps.

Jumpin' Jack Doolin was a daredevil cowboy whose horse did most of the work, while Jack took most of the credit. One day the horse stopped short, and Jack found himself at the edge of the Grand Canyon, nearly a mile deep and five miles across. Sure that his horse could leap to the other side, Jack urged him to try it, but the distance was too great—down they plunged. Jack survived because he jumped off at the last minute and "only fell about twenty feet."

Teddy Roosevelt served as a police commissioner in New York City before he became nationally known. Ever the man of action, Roosevelt spent as little time as possible behind a desk, preferring to walk the streets with police officers in order to see the people and their problems close up. Some policemen were so impressed with Teddy's leadership and courage that they volunteered to join his "Rough Riders" in the Spanish-American War of 1898.

Benjamin Franklin was another real person who seemed to be larger than life. Among many other achievements, Franklin literally "stole fire from the gods" during a thunderstorm—bringing electricity down to earth through a kite with a metal key tied to its tail. Though he enjoyed being recognized as a genius, he also liked to emphasize the value of plain living and hard work. Thus he invented his own folk character, "Poor Richard," as a way of giving practical advice to others.

Nature is often larger than life, and characters in folk tales must cope with it as best they can. One dark day in Kansas, for instance, strong winds tore the roof off of Mrs. Hutchinson's house, picked up her kitchen stove, moved it eighty miles away, then came back the next morning for the pots and pans. An eager newspaper reporter trying to follow this story was blown inside out. When Mrs. Hutchinson and her neighbors realized what had happened, they helped the man to turn himself right side out again, then patiently set to work rebuilding their homes.

Many additional tales of characters larger than life can be found in libraries or bookstores. I especially recommend Nathan Miller's *Theodore Roosevelt*, Harold Felton's *Legends of Paul Bunyan*, Lewis Spence's *Myths of the North American Indians*, and Jeanette Faurot's *Asian-Pacific Folktales and Legends*.

OUTLAWS, CROOKS, AND CHEATERS

Black Bart, PO 8

A man who called himself "Charles E. Boles" taught school in the rough-and-tumble mining towns of northern California during the 1870s. He was a short, quiet, well-dressed gentleman who kept mostly to himself, but every once in a while he surprised people with his big toothy smile and his unexpected sense of humor. He just couldn't resist playing practical jokes—not on any of his students, but on another teacher, a friend or acquaintance, sometimes even total strangers—looking dignified and serious as he patiently set the stage. Then, as his victim realized it was a joke, Boles would burst into laughter, slapping his thighs, whooping and hollering like a man gone crazy.

One day his joking went too far. Boles was riding home after school, guiding his gray horse along a rough trail that crossed the main road, when he saw a Wells Fargo stagecoach coming slowly towards him up the mountain. He knew the driver and decided it would be fun to scare the fellow a little. So Boles hid his horse behind some mesquite bushes, broke off a crooked branch to pretend he had a gun, tied a bandana over his mouth, and stepped out into the road as the stage approached. It stopped abruptly.

"Throw down your money box!" Boles shouted.

The driver, surprised and frightened, did just that, and the big box burst open when it hit the ground beside the road, spilling out golden bars and bags of gold dust. No telling how much it might be worth! As Boles examined this treasure, forgetting to reveal who he was, the driver yelled at the horses and the stagecoach rolled away.

Boles started packing the gold back into the box, thinking he could catch up with the stagecoach and explain his joke to the driver and passengers. Then he thought some more. He might have to teach school for two more years to earn as much money as this gold was worth—why not just keep it? Stealing was wrong, but being poor didn't seem to be exactly the right idea either. Boles quickly stuffed the gold into his own saddlebags and rode off, leaving the empty box behind. So began his new and more exciting career as a bandit.

When he got home to his rented wooden shanty, Boles did what a lot of people in those parts did—he pried up one of the floorboards to make a hiding place. Under it he placed a small sack of gold dust, an old watch that didn't tell good time, and other odds and ends. He was tempted to add some kind of a funny note for any robber who might come along, but then he thought it might be better to leave well enough alone. The rest of the gold he buried out in the brush in several different locations, which he memorized before he did another thing.

During the next seven years, Charles Boles held up more than thirty Wells Fargo stagecoaches, mostly in the mining country of northern California. Some drivers were braver than others, some stagecoaches carried armed guards as well, but Boles always

managed to take them by surprise, usually at a spot where the stage was climbing a steep hill or starting to cross a stream. He never fired a shot, and never got caught. Well, almost never—the Pinkerton detectives did catch up with him, but that was later on.

Compared to other outlaws, Boles was probably luckier and smarter than most. He planned every detail in advance, and was careful about disguising himself and hiding his tracks. But he couldn't resist a joke. After each robbery of a stagecoach, he would leave a humorous note in the empty money box. For example:

"This is my way to get money and bread.
When I have a chance why should I refuse it?
I'll not need either when I'm dead,
And I only tax those who are able to lose it.

"So blame me not for what I've done,
I don't deserve your curses;
And if for some cause I must be hung,
Let it be for my verses."

He signed these poetic notes with a name that was also a joke: *"Black Bart, Po8."*

Not long after Black Bart the poet began holding up stagecoaches, Charles E. Boles the schoolteacher quit his job and disappeared from the mining town where he had been working. Coincidentally, a prosperous and well-dressed gentleman who used the name "C. E. Bolton" arrived in San Francisco, and let it be known that his prosperity came from gold mines up in the mountains, which he had to visit periodically. Nobody connected Bolton with Boles, or either one of those two with Black Bart, and it was only by chance that the poetry-writing bandit was finally caught. The vital clue to his identity was discovered because of the brave actions of a fifteen-year-old boy named Jimmy Roleri.

On a fine November day in 1883, near the Stanislaus River, Black Bart held up the stagecoach in which Jimmy Roleri was coming back from a visit to his grandparents. As usual, the driver threw the money box down for Bart without a fight, but this time it didn't break open. Smash! Bart attacked the box, using a heavy sledgehammer and chisel that he always carried with him, just in case. The box was full of gold, as usual, and Bart lost no time loading it into the saddlebags of his nearby horse. He needed only two or three minutes to do all of this. Then he put his usual note in the money box and climbed onto his horse.

When Jimmy realized what was happening, he slipped out the other side of the coach and crouched behind it, taking the new .22-caliber single-shot rifle he had been given for his birthday. Just as Black Bart was starting to ride away, Jimmy aimed the rifle and fired his one shot.

Bart was hit in the arm or hand. He lost his derby hat as he galloped off. Also a detachable white cuff, spotted with blood, fell from the sleeve of his shirt.

At last the Pinkertons, the detectives who worked for Wells Fargo, had some clues to follow. The derby hat didn't help much because they couldn't tell who owned it. But the shirt cuff, made of expensive white linen, had been marked

"FXO7" by a commercial laundry somewhere to identify a particular customer. Find that laundry, and they would have their man!

More than three dozen Pinkerton detectives spread out across northern California, looking for the laundry that had marked someone's shirt that way. No luck in the mining towns, where most people did their own washing or did without. No luck in nearby cities such as Sacramento, where the Chinese laundrymen marked things in their own language.

So the detectives spread out further, some going as far as Las Vegas and Los Angeles. Finally, in San Francisco, the detectives found a laundry that recognized the "FXO7" mark and identified the owner: Mr. C. E. Bolton, who resided at an elegant private hotel, the Webb House, not far away.

The rest was easy. Having stationed several of his best men in the hallway and outside the window, Pinkerton's chief detective knocked on the door of Bolton's room, carrying a bundle of clean shirts from the laundry, as though he were making a delivery. When Bolton started to pay him, the detective interrupted.

"I think this may also be yours, Bart."

The detective handed him the blood-spotted cuff which had led the Pinkertons to him. Bart was surprised, but he had to laugh, too, because this time the joke was on him.

Bolton/Bart/Boles served six years in San Quentin prison for armed robbery. That was the end of his poetry, but his story wasn't quite finished. Soon after he was released, a mysterious bandit began holding up the Wells Fargo stagecoaches that carried gold from the mines in the mountains. This bandit took the drivers by surprise, never firing a shot, and always getting away.

No notes were left in the boxes this time, but the detectives were pretty sure they knew who was doing it. So they found him again in San Francisco and had a friendly chat. Bart said that he wasn't getting any younger. Actually he would like to retire from this kind of work, if he could be assured of enough money to live on.

"How about a monthly payment from the company?" he asked.

Bart may have meant this as a joke, but the detectives took it seriously. Three days later, Wells Fargo agreed to pay him a generous pension each month, for the rest of his life, if he would promise to stop robbing them. Bart gave his word, shook hands on the deal, and that was the end of his story.

Jesse James and the Widow

One of the strangest things about Jesse James, the man who robbed so many banks and trains during the 1870s, was that he didn't know what to do with his share of the money. He bought fast horses for himself and kept a few dollars to live on, but he gave a lot away. "Easy come, easy go," Jesse used to say.

It surely was easy to get money, as the James gang became known and feared in Missouri, Kansas, Arkansas, and beyond. It was easy to get rid of money, too, when Jesse began helping those in need. Widows and orphans, for instance. Small farmers down on their luck. Army veterans who couldn't find work. To many of these good people, Jesse James must have seemed like a hero more than a thief—they wouldn't listen to a word spoken against him.

Jesse's favorite widow was a woman he met in October, 1871, just after he and his brother Frank held up a stagecoach in Fayetteville, Arkansas. As they were riding out of town, with nobody pursuing them, Jesse said it would be nice to stop and have a hot meal somewhere. Frank agreed. They swung away from the main road, onto a trail that led back through the low green hills, and soon came to a tidy-looking cabin with smoke rising from the chimney.

Jesse knocked. A woman came to the door, holding a handkerchief to her face. "Who is it?"

As Jesse explained that the brothers wanted a good meal, and would pay her well for it, Frank studied the woman carefully. She was wearing a black dress. Her dark hair

had vivid streaks of white. She didn't seem all that old, but her cheeks were wet with tears as though she had been crying.

"Is something the matter, ma'am?" Frank asked.

"My husband was killed in the war. I haven't been able to collect his pension. Now it's just me and my two children, Stevie and Sue—they're in school down the road—and the mortgage on this farm has to be paid today. The banker is coming here at three o'clock this afternoon. I haven't got the money to pay him!"

She wept again, while the James brothers shifted their feet uncomfortably.

"Ma'am, how much do you owe the bank?" Jesse asked.

"Four hundred dollars, and I haven't got but fifty-two dollars saved up."

Jesse had more than enough money with him, so he offered to lend the widow the full amount she owed.

"And don't worry about paying me back right away," he added. "I'll come around next year, maybe, and that'll be soon enough."

After hearing Jesse's words, the widow perked up quite a bit. She fixed them a good lunch of corn bread and pea soup with plenty of ham scraps. Jesse insisted on paying her ten dollars for the meal, apart from his loan, and the widow accepted. She stood in the doorway as they left, smiling through her tears.

Shortly after three that afternoon, Jesse and Frank took the black-suited banker by surprise as he rode along the trail from the widow's cabin. They had a simple plan—to rob him of the four hundred dollars they had "loaned" the widow to pay off her mortgage. That way, she would own her place free and clear, while they would get the money back to spend or give away again.

The banker climbed stiffly down off his horse. Sure enough, there was a leather satchel strapped behind his saddle—but it was empty.

"Where's your money?" Jesse demanded.

The banker smiled, and twitched his thin black mustache.

"I just spent my money buying a farm back there. If you'll let me reach into my pocket, I'll show you the deed for the property."

"You mean there wasn't any mortgage on the place?" Frank blurted out.

"Not that I'm aware of," the banker replied.

When Jesse and Frank returned to the cabin, it was deserted. The floor had been neatly swept, the dishes were washed, and there was a piece of paper on the kitchen table, weighted down by one silver dollar.

"*Received of Jesse James,*" the paper said, "*Four Hundred & Ten Dollars & No Cents. Signed, Mary Witter. Let this be a lesson to you.*"

Jesse didn't see exactly what the lesson was supposed to be, but he thought about that clever woman for years afterwards, until he got too busy doing other things.

Petticoat Pirates

Mary Adair was a shy child who lived with her grandmother near Cape Hatteras, North Carolina, in the early 1800s. Mary never went to school and seldom looked at books. She loved to play by herself on the lonely beaches, acting out stories her daydreaming granny told her of long ago.

"I am Punky Dillingham," Mary would shout to the sky and the indifferent seagulls. "I have come here to discover the fountain of youth!" And she would dig watery holes in the sand that were soon washed away by the incoming tide.

Mary's favorite game was to dress up in a long cloak and black boots that had once belonged to her grandfather, and pretend to converse with a seagrape bush.

"Sir Waldo Ranleigh at your service, Madam. And you, I presume, must be the Queen of Elizabeth City?"

The seagrape didn't respond, but Mary imagined that the Queen was commanding her to sail the seven seas in search of gold and jewels. All she needed was a ship. She scanned the horizon day after day. The few ships that passed were headed north toward Virginia or south toward Florida—usually they had no reason to come near the shallow waters of the coast where Mary lived.

One day, while Mary was dressed in her cloak and boots, she fell asleep among the seagrape bushes and dreamed that pirates had landed nearby. At least she thought it was a dream. Men's voices could be heard, and laughter, and sounds of digging. When Mary sat up and peeked through the bushes, she saw half a dozen barefooted villains in striped shirts and bell-bottom trousers, with a leader dressed in boots and cloak like hers. The leader also wore a dark wig and a three-cornered hat, which Mary wanted for herself. She straightened her costume and boldly approached the strangers.

"I am Sir Waldo Ranleigh," she began, "and now, Captain, I will have the very hat from your head."

There was a roar of laughter from the pirates, for that is what they were, and the leader smiled, drawing a cutlass and tossing another to Mary.

"Take my hat, then, if you can."

Mary was astonished to hear the voice of a young woman. For once her imagination deserted her.

"But . . . but . . ." she stammered.

"But yourself," the young woman answered, as her crew laughed again. "I'm Jacqueline Caldecott, better known as 'Calico Jack,' the terror of the seas. If you won't fight me for my hat, I've got no use for you."

Still not sure if she was dreaming, Mary swung her borrowed cutlass at the pirate leader, but she was clumsy with it and fell flat on her face in the sand. A foot landed on her back. The sharp point of a sword pricked her neck.

"Yield or die!" said the young woman. "I'll slice you up and plant you with the treasure chest."

"Spare me!" Mary cried loudly, like a character in one of her granny's stories.

The pirates took her prisoner and sailed away in their ship, the *Jack of Diamonds*,

 looking for treasure wherever they could find it. At first they treated Mary as a servant—she washed clothes, helped the cook, polished the boots of Calico Jack. But soon she and Jack became friendly. Sometimes the two of them would dress up in silk dresses and lace petticoats that Jack had found on captured treasure ships. Parading around the deck, they looked like two elegant ladies on a cruise. Other times, Jack taught Mary how to use swords and pistols until she was as skillful as any man.

"Shoot me," Jack said one day, pointing at her own heart.

"I can't," Mary protested.

"Shoot me!" Jack insisted.

Mary took aim, pulled the trigger, and bang! A bright red stain appeared on Jack's white shirt. Mary stood still, said nothing. The pirates laughed uproariously. Jack tore open her shirt and revealed a bulletproof plate of Spanish steel.

"Mary Adair, you've passed a test," cried Jack. "From now on you are one of us, and we shall call you Mary Daring."

So Mary joined the pirates, and lived as they did. From Long Island Sound to the Gulf of Mexico, tales were told about her many daring deeds. There were days when she thought she must be dreaming, and nights when she was sure she was awake.

The Arkansas Traveler

Sandy Faulkner moved from Kentucky to Arkansas in 1829 and settled in Chicot County, on the Mississippi River, as a cotton planter. With his polished Southern manners and refined appearance, young Faulkner made friends easily among the sophisticated families owning large farms near his, and he enjoyed the lively parties and dances to which they invited him. It was a limited community, to be sure, but surprisingly up-to-date in news, music, fashions, so he seldom regretted his decision to settle there.

As the years went by, however, Sandy Faulkner felt increasingly curious about the other Arkansas—the back country and the Ozark Mountains, where clusters of poor whites and blacks were said to live in total isolation from the outside world. He wanted to see this for himself. Therefore he was pleased to join a small number of gentlemen who traveled to the farthest corners of the state during the political campaign of 1840, seeking support for President Martin Van Buren against a strong challenger.

Faulkner became separated from his traveling companions in a rainstorm west of Little Rock, but he decided to press on regardless, wet and cold, because the most interesting places lay ahead of him, and his horse was still fresh. At a remote crossroads called "Lost Corner" in the Ozarks, he thought he might dry himself off and stay the night. Perhaps he could even say a few words about the President. His audience wasn't large—a bearded man sitting on a stump beside a shack, a woman banging pots inside, five or six children peering like possums from the shadows. The man was busy tuning a fiddle, but he looked up when Faulkner approached.

"Hello, my good fellow," Faulkner began.

"Hello yourself," the bearded man replied sourly.

"Sir, can I get to stay the night?" the traveler continued.

"No, Sir, you surely can't get there from here."

"Well, how about something for dinner?"

"Nice of you to offer, Mister, but I just et."

"I'm hungry, haven't had a bite since morning—can't you give me anything to eat?"

"Hain't a thing left in the house, not a morsel of meat nor a dust of corn meal."

"Well, how far is it to the next house?"

"Don't rightly know, I never been there."

"So I'll have to stay in your house tonight, won't I?"

"Well, Sir, my house leaks."

"Why don't you stop it from leaking?"

"It's been rainin' all day."

"Well, why don't you fix it in dry weather?"

"It don't leak then."

At this point the bearded man began fiddling a scratchy tune which drew the children out to caper in the yard. Inside the shack, the banging of pots had ceased. Faulkner breathed deeply, rejoicing, looking at the jolly, unspoiled children and the high woods surrounding them—this was the country he had come to see!

When the bearded fiddler stopped playing, Faulkner asked if he could try, and offered the same tune himself, a little slower but with more polish.

"Well I'll be danged!" the bearded man exclaimed. "You never said you war a fiddler, stranger."

"Not as good as you," the traveler replied. "But now, Sir, how about a night's lodging in your house? Name your price."

"Why not?" said the man. "Give me a twenty-dollar gold piece and go on inside, while I see to your horse."

Faulkner entered the shack and sat down at the table, hoping to be fed. He was surprised when the middle-aged woman looked at him strangely and refused to let him stay.

"But, Madam, I paid your husband quite handsomely to sleep in this house," the traveler protested.

"No, Sir, you never did," said the woman.

"But he—"

"He ain't my husband, and this ain't his house."

"You mean I've been misled?" the traveler gasped.

"I don't know nothin' about that," the woman responded, "but you sure as heck been Ozarked."

Steve Brodie Jumps Off the Brooklyn Bridge

Steve Brodie graduated from high school in June, 1885, and couldn't find a decent job. For six months he washed dishes at a busy restaurant on Broadway while he looked around. Then he began working at The Museum of Many Wonders near the Manhattan end of the Brooklyn Bridge. Dressed in a purple-and-white striped suit, his hair slicked down with grease, Steve stood outside and tried to persuade people to go inside, reciting a list of the amazing things they would see *"for one thin dime, the tenth part of a dollar."* Dinosaur bones and unicorn horns, pieces of Abraham Lincoln's log cabin, a bald eagle's feathers, some ribbons from Queen Victoria's wedding dress—the list went on and on.

Many of these wonders existed only in the imagination of Steve's greedy boss, Mr. DeWitt. The museum was really just a warehouse filled with old junk, but his customers didn't know that until it was too late. If they came out and demanded their ten cents back, DeWitt showed them the very small sign that said ABSOLUTELY NO REFUNDS. A dime was worth somewhat more in those days than it is now, but most people didn't argue with DeWitt. They just shrugged and walked away.

Steve hated this job—yet he kept asking himself what else could he do? Times were tough, and he needed the money to help support his mother and sisters. So he worked day after day, reciting DeWitt's list of wonders over and over, until he didn't have to think about it any more. His mind drifted off to more pleasant things—doing

something important, becoming famous and rich, getting married to the girl of his dreams. He didn't yet know who this girl might be, but he could picture her as he stood on the sidewalk all day long: black hair piled up on top of her head, sparkling blue or green eyes, a special smile just for him—and smart as a whip. Yes, indeed. With a smart wife to steer him, there was no telling where a promising young fellow like Steve Brodie might go!

July 4, 1886, was the hottest day Steve could remember. He suffered inside his heavy striped suit. There were very few customers as most people stayed home or went to Coney Island to swim. The hours dragged by. Steve asked Mr. DeWitt to close the museum early, but it was no use. DeWitt wanted every last dime he could squeeze out of the unsuspecting public.

"You're not tough enough for show business," he sneered at Steve. "If it's too hot for you, why don't you go and take a flying leap from the Brooklyn Bridge? That should cool you off!"

"Oh yeah?" Steve shouted back at him. "I'll show you who's tough."

Steve left the museum and ran through the sweltering streets to the Brooklyn Bridge. It soared above him, its steel cables shimmering in the heat. He rushed up the walkway to the bridge's highest point, and looked down at the swirling currents of the East River. Such a long way to jump!

"I can't do it," he admitted to himself. But he didn't want to give DeWitt the satisfaction of knowing this, so he rushed down to the river's edge, plunged in, and splashed around for a few moments. The cool, smelly water felt wonderful. Then he hurried back to the museum, his suit dripping, and caught DeWitt by surprise.

"I did it, you see? Don't tell me who's tough!"

DeWitt didn't believe him at first, but Steve kept insisting. So DeWitt had a new sign made. Now Steve greeted people in his bathing suit, introducing himself as *"the only man who ever jumped off the Brooklyn Bridge and lived to tell about it."*

Steve lived with this lie for more than two weeks. The newspapers wrote about it, and people came to the museum just to meet him. He was going strong until July 23, when he was approached by a tall young woman with black hair piled up on top of her head, sparkling green eyes, and a smile that thrilled him.

"I'm writing a story about you for *Harper's Weekly*," she said. "Will you tell me exactly what happened?"

Steve looked at her, and saw his future.

"Yes, of course, but there's something I've got to do first," he replied. "Will you please wait right here?"

Judge Roy Bean and His Pet Bear

In the 1880s a middle-aged Texan named Henry "Hank" Ketchum decided to try cattle rustling. He had been honest up to that point, working in a general store near Houston, but the store went out of business and Hank couldn't find another job, so he thought he would steal a few head of cattle and sell them for whatever he could get. Maybe he'd use that money to move to Oklahoma and start over.

Hank saddled his broken-down horse one evening, and rode out across the prairie to the nearest ranch, figuring that the owners would never miss half a dozen steers on a dark night. He swung his rope around and around in a big loop, as he had seen fellers do in rodeos, and then flung it in the direction of the nearest steer. Or what looked like a steer. Actually it was a horse belonging to the ranch foreman, who was taking his turn at guarding the herd. Hank's long rope hit the foreman smack in the face, knocking his hat off and raising a lump on his forehead.

"What in tarnation?" the foreman cried. He pulled his gun, squinted in Hank's direction, fired a couple of shots, and quickly put an end to Hank's career as a cattle rustler. Tied up in his own rope and prodded by the ranch foreman, Hank was forced to walk the two miles back into town, wishing he could find a way out of the trouble he was in.

But the Texas laws about stealing cattle were pretty clear and simple in those days. They were especially clear and simple in that particular part of Texas, where "Judge" Roy Bean decided who was guilty of what. Roy Bean was also a saloon-keeper, but he had studied the law somewhere, and he had two thick law books that he used to quote from. Since there was no other judge for many miles around, lots of folks brought their legal problems to him.

Judge Bean's courtroom consisted of two long planks resting on two empty barrels, with a glass of whisky close to his left hand and a Colt .44 revolver next to his right. When Hank Ketchum was brought before him, the Judge had nothing better to do, so he listened attentively to every detail of the case, from both sides, and then made his decision.

"Guilty of cattle rustling as charged," he said. "Mister Ketchum, you are hereby fined five dollars, and sentenced to death by hanging. That's my ruling."

Judge Bean was just about to adjourn the court—when suddenly a better idea occurred to him.

"A plea for clemency has been entered," said the Judge. "Your sentence is hereby reduced to thirty days of animal husbandry." Having no gavel, the Judge banged the handle of his pistol on the wooden counter, and that was that.

Hank didn't know who or what clemency was, and he wasn't sure about husbandry—yet it sounded a lot better than hanging, so he politely thanked the judge and followed him outside.

Behind the saloon a huge, shaggy, unhappy-looking brown bear lived in what used to be a corral for horses. Hank understood that he was going to live there, too. The bear came over to the gate, sniffed at Hank, and waited as the Judge put Hank inside.

"This here is Lily, the light of my life," said the Judge. "Feed her and brush her coat for thirty days, sing her a song now and then, and your time will be up before you can say skid-doo!"

Hank soon adjusted to his new life, eating when Lily ate, sleeping when she slept, and singing her songs he had learned in the Army, such as "Marching Through Georgia" and "Camptown Races." The bear especially liked marching around and around the corral, following Hank as he sang.

After four weeks of this, the Judge was so pleased that he added another thirty days to the sentence, and Hank realized he might be stuck there forever. The next moonless night, he climbed out of the corral to freedom. Lily followed him, naturally. The two of them walked away unchallenged, disappearing into the darkness of the prairie as they headed for the distant hills. Lily found a cave there, but Hank kept going for several weeks, until he stumbled into the unclaimed oil fields of Oklahoma and struck it rich.

The Plan to Saw Off Manhattan

Bertrand Charpentier came to New York from Paris as a child, in 1798, because his father had been killed in the French Revolution, and his terrified mother could think only to flee.

Their voyage was a nightmare. The ship, a rotten old hulk that should have been scrapped years earlier, seemed to be sinking. There was no fresh water and little food. Bertrand's mother, shuddering with fever, died during the fourth week. Bertrand sat beside her body, day and night, as waves broke over the deck and other people screamed. When he finally landed in Manhattan, Bertrand was starving, friendless, disconnected from the world around him.

He understood no English, but kept repeating his name "Charpentier." Eventually someone took him to a building on Mulberry Street, where several carpenters shared a workshop. Two of them, Canadians, spoke French with Bertrand and hired him as an apprentice—sandpapering boards, straightening bent nails, and sweeping up sawdust. He was usually too busy or too tired to think much, but at night he had terrible dreams—Paris on fire, his mother screaming, his father being dragged away, the hurried trip from Paris to Normandy, the old ship sinking, the water lapping at his legs as he held his mother's cold hand.

Years passed. Bertrand learned some English and a little arithmetic but he never went to school, nor did he make any close friends outside the small circle of carpenters. When he was eighteen, they gave him a toolbox of his own. Bertrand began to make furniture.

Then one day a well-dressed stranger came into the workshop. He spoke English with a French accent. He said that he wanted to hire carpenters for special work.

"What kind of special work?" said one of the Canadians. "A bigger palace for the Mayor?"

"No, nothing of the kind," the stranger replied. "I represent a group of investors who wish to saw Manhattan off from the rest of New York, so that . . . "

"Are you crazy?" the Canadian shouted.

"Not at all," said the man. "And please allow me to continue. The problem is that Manhattan has too many people living at the southern end, and not enough at the northern end, so it's in serious danger of tilting suddenly, like a sinking ship, and causing thousands of innocent families to drown, unless . . . "

"And you, my friend, are in serious danger of receiving a kick in the pants," the Canadian responded, "unless you get out of here and take your nonsense somewhere else. Everybody knows that Manhattan is an island of solid rock!"

"No nonsense, no nonsense," the man spluttered, but he left abruptly, and the carpenters returned to work. They didn't notice that Bertrand slipped out the door and followed the man down the street.

"I am a carpenter," he said timidly. "I will help."

"Of course you will," the man said, and as they walked he explained his plan in great detail, not much of which poor Bertrand understood.

However, Bertrand had some acquaintances among the workmen and apprentices of that neighborhood, and he spread the word to them, handing out notices of a public meeting to be held that evening at the very tip of Manhattan, in Battery Park. *Do a Big Job for Big Pay,* the notices said, *Bring Your Tools!*

When the meeting started, the well-dressed man was nowhere to be seen. Hundreds of people waited impatiently. So Bertrand stood up on a railing, with his back to the splendid harbor, and repeated the few words that he knew, over and over, louder and louder, until he could speak no more.

"If we don't saw off Manhattan, it will sink, because of the weight, like a ship!"

Most people realized this was impossible, and laughed about it. But others were angry and blamed Bertrand, crowding around him, shouting and shoving, until he fell over backwards, rolled down the slippery stones of the sea wall, and plunged into the deep, chilly water.

Suddenly the fear of drowning went through his body like an electric shock! His mind cleared! With a great effort, Bertrand fought his way up to the surface, struggled ashore, and ran soaking through the streets to his room above the carpentry shop.

That night, for the first time, Bertrand had pleasant dreams. The next morning he gathered his few belongings, parted company with the carpenters, and went looking for a friendly ship to take him home to France.

Endless Herd of Cattle

In August 1880, a businessman named Angus McDill traveled all the way from Scotland to Wyoming to buy cattle. He was a sharp trader, but he had been warned that some of the Americans might be sharp, too, so he brought with him a keen-eyed little bookkeeper to count every dollar and every steer. He also brought a fierce-looking bagpiper, dressed in a plaid kilt, and a gallon of very powerful Scotch whiskey.

McDill was going to meet a rancher by the name of Jake Dorsey, who had offered to sell 5,000 cattle for $25 a head—the lowest price around. Before McDill's arrival, Dorsey made plans with his ranch foreman, Buck.

"Scotchmen are rich," Dorsey explained, "and this here letter says they want to pay cash. So our only problem is how to make our small herd of cattle look like it's almost endless."

Buck waited. He knew from past experience that Dorsey would find a solution.

"I've got it!" Dorsey exclaimed. "Buck, you know that pint-sized mountain up at the north end of the ranch, with a narrow canyon along side of it? Here's what I want you to do. . . ."

Saturday morning Dorsey's guests arrived. He loaded them into a wagon and drove them out across the range towards the place he had in mind. Except for a few pieces of tumbleweed blowing in the wind, the vast landscape was dry-looking and empty. It would soon be hot from the sun.

"I dinna see verra many cattle," said Angus McDill.

"Oh, they're mostly back in the hills, behind that mountain," said Dorsey. "It's cooler there, and the grazing is better."

When they got close to the small mountain, Dorsey drove part way up the canyon beside it, where he could park the wagon on a broad ledge under the shade of some pine trees.

"We'll set right here," he explained. "I'll have Buck and the boys drive the cattle past us, and you can count 'em to your heart's content."

"Are they healthy, all of them?" McDill asked.

"Why sure, as far as I know," Dorsey replied. "But if you happen to see one or two head you don't like the looks of, just holler and we'll cut them out of the herd."

Soon the noise of thundering hooves came rolling down the narrow canyon, and the leading steers appeared, followed by dozens of others in a growing cloud of dust. Several of Dorsey's cowboys rode among them. It was difficult to see, but Angus McDill was pleased. These steers were big! Much bigger than the Scottish cattle he was used to. Buying them here at $25 each, he could sell them for a substantial profit back in Aberdeen. He tried not to show his pleasure. Instead he poured out a round of Scotch whiskey and told the bagpiper to give them a tune. Meanwhile the herd disappeared in the dust.

"How many is that so far?" McDill asked the bookkeeper.

"Four hundred and ninety-nine," was the reply.

"That's funny," said Dorsey. "We keep them separated into batches of five hundred, and I was sure I was giving you a true count."

A moment later, an old yellow steer came walking slowly down the canyon by himself, looking tired and ready for a rest.

"There you go," said Dorsey, "that one makes it an even five hundred."

"Nay, but he's not fit like the others," McDill objected. "I canna pay you annathin' for him."

"Then we'll take him away," said Dorsey, "and give you five hundred and one in the next batch."

Again the noise of thundering hooves came down the narrow canyon, as cattle appeared in a cloud of dust. The bookkeeper counted, the bagpiper played, and Dorsey had another wee sip of Scotch whiskey. He smiled—his plan was working exactly as he had hoped.

McDill was smiling too, until his bookkeeper told him the count for this second herd of cattle.

"Four hundred and ninety-nine," the man reported.

"Are ye sure?" McDill demanded. "Go over your tallies again for me, there's a good man."

While the bookkeeper was checking his numbers, an old yellow steer came walking slowly down the canyon by himself, looking tired and ready for a rest.

"Why, that's the same poor beast we saw before," said McDill. "I'm almost certain of it."

"No, that's a different one," said Dorsey. "I could go down and check his brand to make sure, but I tell you what—we won't count him either. Fair enough?"

McDill agreed. After a short pause, the sound of thundering hooves was heard

again, and cattle started coming through the narrow canyon at a trot. When they were finished, McDill looked over at Dorsey.

"Four hundred and ninety and nine," the little bookkeeper cried excitedly. "Again, you're short by one!"

As Dorsey tried to think of something clever to say, an old yellow steer came walking slowly down the canyon by himself, looking tired and ready for a rest.

"What d'ye tell me this time?" asked McDill. "Is it the same beast or no?"

"Can't be," said Dorsey. "That one is miles away by now. But I'll check on it. You eat some lunch and get ready for the next batch of steers."

Dorsey unhitched one of the horses from his wagon, and rode quickly up the canyon to find Buck before anything else went wrong. While he was gone, McDill had a quiet talk with his bookkeeper and his bagpiper. It was time for a new idea.

When Dorsey returned, the piper was playing a Scottish tune, "The Campbells Are Coming," and the bookkeeper was sharpening his pencil with a pocketknife.

"Are we ready for the next batch?" said Dorsey.

"Indeed we are," McDill replied. He poured another wee whiskey for Dorsey, and waited as the sound of thundering cattle came down the canyon again. They trotted past in twos and threes and fours. When the last of them had disappeared through the dust, McDill's bookkeeper announced the total.

"Four hundred ninety-seven."

"Agreed?" McDill asked Dorsey.

"Agreed."

All that Saturday afternoon they continued to watch cattle go by, and the bookkeeper called out the totals: 498, 497, 495, 491, and so on. Never exactly five hundred. And the old yellow steer was not

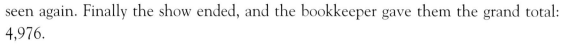

seen again. Finally the show ended, and the bookkeeper gave them the grand total: 4,976.

"Not the five thousand I came for, Mr. Dorsey," said McDill.

"No, not exactly, but you're bound to lose a few along the way. I'm glad to accept your count, and the price still stands—twenty-five dollars a head. I got the bill of sale right here, ready to fill in and sign. How you move 'em after this is up to you."

"Perfectly satisfactory," said McDill. "My bookkeeper will count out the money for you. It's all in Scottish sovereigns if you don't mind. Solid gold coins and any American bank will accept them."

"Sounds okay to me," Dorsey said.

"As you count your coins," McDill continued, "the piper will help you to stuff them back into my own leather satchel, which is yours to keep, since I won't be needing it any more."

"Why that's mighty nice of you, Mr. McDill," said Dorsey. "I do know gold when I see it, but I never expected to handle so much of it all in one place."

The Scotsman and the rancher smiled at each other, shook hands, filled in the blanks and signed the paper, which said that Jacob Dorsey had sold Angus McDill 4,976 head of cattle for the sum of $124,400.

Dorsey took each gold coin from McDill, and passed it along to the bagpiper, who was holding the leather satchel open on his lap, next to his bagpipes. Dorsey could hear the clinking of coins, and he assumed the gold was dropping into the satchel. But he was tired and hot and a little fuzzy from drinking so many sips of Scotch whiskey, so he did not watch everything as carefully as he might have. When Dorsey finally picked up the satchel, however, it felt very heavy, and he thought he could hear the clink of gold against gold inside.

Dorsey and Buck drove their visitors back to town, assuring them it would be easy to make arrangements for rounding up their endless herd of cattle the following week. That would give Dorsey time to deposit the contents of his leather satchel in the bank, after which he intended to vanish.

They all shook hands and said farewell. Then, as the three Scotsmen walked towards the entrance of their hotel, the piper began to play a final tune—very faint, very slow, very dull. It sounded as though his leather bagpipes were now full of something besides warm air.

"That's mighty strange music they're playing," said Buck.

"Well, the Scotch are mighty strange people," Dorsey replied. "They think they know it all, of course, but maybe this time we outsmarted them."

Frankie & Johnnie

Frances Ernestine Baker, known as Frankie to her friends, was one of the restless young people of color who drifted into St. Louis, Missouri, during the 1890s. St. Louis was a turbulent place in those days—less violent than Tombstone, Abilene, and other gunfighting towns of the Wild West, but still tough, fast-moving, tricky, and often dangerous. Frankie learned this the hard way soon after her arrival. Looking for work at a downtown restaurant, she said something that sounded insulting to one of the waitresses. *Owww!* Faster than the eye could follow, a straight razor slashed Frankie's right cheek. With blood running down her pretty brown face, Frankie wasted no time on tears. She found a barbershop nearby, paid the man to patch her up, and bought a folding razor to protect herself.

Although she was smart and ambitious, Frankie couldn't get a decent job after that. Restaurants, stores, offices all turned her away because of her ugly scar. She might have worked in a kitchen or a stockroom, out of sight, but she was too proud to hide her face. Instead she made the rounds of the dance halls, the saloons, and finally the gambling parlors. At the biggest and best of these she was greeted with open arms by the fat black man who handled the money.

"I don't know a thing about card games," Frankie admitted.

"This you can learn, honey, this you can learn," he replied. "But you got something else that nobody could teach you, and it's called class."

He was right. Even before Frankie became an expert at dealing poker, blackjack, and other games of chance, she began to attract customers with her unusual good looks, her quick wit, and her air of being above it all.

"I'm here because we're having fun," she seemed to say, "not because I have to be."

Men and women, black and white, crowded around Frankie's table to share in the ups and downs of the game—whether they won or lost. "Some of my biggest winners are losers," Frankie would declare, laughing, and the players would laugh with her. They thought they understood what she meant.

What Frankie really meant, though, was that she was getting hooked—not on liquor or drugs or gambling, but on gamblers. She was developing a weakness for men who bet everything they had, or more than they had, and lost it all, then came back the next night or the next week and started all over again. She met a lot of men like that, since there were a lot of them around, not only in St. Louis but also in Chicago, New Orleans, Denver, Omaha and other cities with plenty of easy money, where fortunes changed hands often. Win tonight, lose tomorrow, win the day after, lose the night after that, and so on.

These sporting men, and the women who traveled with them, began to regard Frankie Baker as the queen of their kind. "See you at Frankie's," they'd say to one another, though she didn't own the Twelfth Street gambling parlor where she worked, and her name wasn't on the sign over the door. She simply dominated the scene with her skill and humor from the moment that

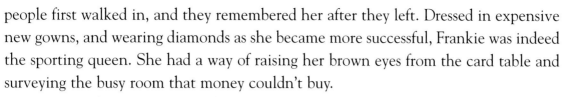

people first walked in, and they remembered her after they left. Dressed in expensive new gowns, and wearing diamonds as she became more successful, Frankie was indeed the sporting queen. She had a way of raising her brown eyes from the card table and surveying the busy room that money couldn't buy.

Into Frankie's view one night swept a man who caught her interest immediately. Tall, dark, and wolfishly handsome, the legendary Jean E. Beauregard had arrived from New Orleans earlier that day with a satchel full of dollars and the devil in his heart. He had heard about Frankie's establishment from other gamblers on the steamboat

coming up the Mississippi, and he entered like a king—brisk, sure of himself, seemingly certain that people would make way before him.

Frankie and Beauregard spotted each other as the gamblers cleared away from her table. Electricity passed between them. Frankie asked him what he wanted to play, and Beauregard smiled at her wordlessly for a long moment. Frankie, cool as she usually was, felt the pulse thudding in her chest.

"Poker," he said finally, in a voice like music. As there were no other players at the moment, Frankie dealt the cards to play against him, one on one. She was ready to match his skill and daring, but the game was not as challenging as she had hoped. Beauregard kept staring at her instead of paying attention to the cards. He bet large sums carelessly, almost as though he wanted to throw his money away, and within half an hour his leather satchel was empty of dollars. He left the table a loser that night, but they both knew he had won Frankie's heart.

Johnnie Beauregard came back two weeks later with his satchel full of money again, wearing the most outrageous clothes that Frankie had ever seen. Long, flat-heeled shoes with mirrors set in the toes. Black velvet trousers, vest, and hat—Stetson's special "high roller." Embroidered shirt with diamond cuff links, more diamonds on rings, a watch ribbon, sleeve garters. And a loose silk coat, green like Johnnie's eyes, which almost concealed the two pearl-handled pistols he wore holstered under either arm.

"Won my clothes back from a fellow in New Orleans," he told Frankie. "Maybe changed my luck."

In the weeks that followed, Johnnie won and lost a lot of money at her table, but Frankie hardly noticed. She was madly in love with him, and she couldn't wait until the gambling parlor closed at three or four A.M. Then Johnnie would take her out to eat, to go dancing, and kiss her as though he had personally invented romance. If there had been anybody back home to write to, Frankie would have sent them a message of triumph. But she was on her own now, so she had to be content with singing to herself.

Then came a night when Johnnie didn't show up at Frankie's establishment, although he had won big the night before. Frankie, losing her cool for once, asked people if they had seen him, but nobody had. So she made the rounds as soon as she got out of work—Twelfth Street, Carr, Targee, Pine Street—many a man, and some she knew, but no Johnnie. As she was going home through a quiet residential neighborhood, she heard his laugh and, turning, saw him going into an elegant house with another woman. Frankie didn't stop to think. She pushed open the door behind them, drew her razor, and cut Johnnie so badly that he could only whisper to her in anguish.

"My sister," he said faintly, and Frankie could hear nothing after that, not even the screams of the horrified woman who shrank away from her in the hallway.

Stumbling out, Frankie wandered the streets in search of a policeman to confess her crime. But she never stood trial for killing Johnnie Beauregard, who had been wanted for several murders himself. Several months later she returned to work, outwardly the same as before, inwardly a different woman. She had sworn to give her heart to no man, and she kept her word until August, 1899, when Albert Britt appeared beside her table to serve drinks. He was black, slender, poorly dressed, about thirty years old, so shy that he could barely look at Frankie when she spoke to him. But when she saw his green eyes, full of fear and wonder, she was reminded of Johnnie Beauregard at the moment of death, and her heart thudded resoundingly as it had then.

"Four dollars," Albert stammered. "Don't mean to interrupt."

"No, the drinks are free at this table," Frankie replied gently. "I'll explain to you later."

Although she was several years younger than he was, Frankie felt protective towards Albert at first. He seemed so helpless and unsure of himself—the losingest loser she had ever met—and she felt bound to shield him from a world whose dangers he barely recognized. She moved him into her comfortable home, and fed and clothed him lavishly.

"No need for you to work," she said. "I've got more than enough for both of us."

Albert enjoyed this life of leisure for a while. He lived well, and put on some weight, but he had nothing to do all day while Frankie slept, nor most of the night while she dealt cards. So he got bored, and he began cheating on Frankie with one woman after another. When she found out, she used his own pearl-handled pistol to shoot him fatally.

"I loved you," he gasped. "I was your man."

"But you done me wrong," Frankie responded, watching his green eyes close before she was led away.

Captain Kidd

William Kidd, captain of his own ship, brought a mixed cargo of furniture and household goods from London to New York in 1696. He was an unpleasant-looking man with a fiery temper, but he had a reputation for dependability and courage that impressed the merchants of the day. "Kidd will deliver," they'd say, "if anybody can."

After leaving some official papers in the harbormaster's office, Kidd walked slowly up Broadway towards the inn where he intended to stay until his return to England. Lost in thought, he was surprised to find his way suddenly blocked by two British soldiers in red coats. An officer came forward to greet him.

"Captain Kidd? I am Colonel Robert Livingston. His Excellency the Governor wishes to see you at once."

It seemed to be more of an order than an invitation, so Kidd followed Livingston to the brick building that housed the royal governors of this British colony. Governor "Belly" Bellamont, a distant relation of King William, was just completing an enormous meal—either a very late lunch or a very early dinner. Shoving the empty dishes aside before his servants could remove them, Bellamont spread a map on the table and pointed his fork at the middle of it.

"Nova Scotia," he bellowed. "Part of Canada now. Ever been there, Kidd?"

"It's said to be the haunt of pirates," Captain Kidd replied cautiously.

"Precisely, precisely," the Governor snapped. "Bloody scoundrels seize our cargoes, sink our ships, then sail away to Canada and hide their loot on some confounded island."

"Why do you ask me about it?" Kidd persisted.

"We have a proposition for you," the Governor replied. "Tell him, Livingston."

The Colonel explained that a group of investors wanted to arm a suitable ship and send it north to recover stolen property from the pirates in Canada. Other pirates might be captured along the way. A trustworthy leader was needed and Kidd, they thought, was just the man.

"But I have a ship of my own," Kidd objected, "and contracts with merchants back in England. I sail in a week's time."

"There'll be some difficulty with your clearance papers, I imagine," said Livingston smoothly. "Your ship may be tied up here indefinitely."

"You can't do this to me," Kidd shouted angrily.

But their stony looks and their silence told him that they could. Later that evening they forced him to sign his name to a lengthy document he wasn't even allowed to read.

"Never fear," the Governor assured him. "The King himself has graciously agreed to invest in this venture, and you will sail as a privateer with his royal pennant flying from your mast."

A privateer was a heavily armed vessel, privately owned, with a government license to steal. Captain Kidd had no desire to embark on such a voyage, but he was trapped, so he decided to make the best of it. He inspected the investors' ship, supplied it for a year's voyage, and assembled a crew of ruffians and rejects from the Royal Navy. They were misfits, but he could make them do his bidding, and the ship was soon ready for departure.

Leaving the dock, getting back to sea, Captain Kidd felt a momentary sense of freedom. As he sailed north from New York, however, his fierce anger rose again. Having nobody else to take it out on, he bullied his crew day after day, and he ordered them to attack any foreign ship that crossed his path—whether it was under the command of pirates or not. Many innocent vessels were captured in this way. Men were thrown overboard, women and children were mistreated, and cabins were hastily searched for gold, silver, jewels. The year that Kidd had planned to be away became two years, then three.

Finally he wearied of this strange new life, and arranged to meet Colonel Livingston secretly at Montauk, Long Island. Kidd was rowed ashore with four big treasure chests, which he turned over to Livingston. Having kept his bargain with the investors who had hired him, the Captain thought he was finished with them. But when he returned to London he was arrested and charged with piracy. Some of the investors actually testified against him, to cover their own tracks, and Captain Kidd had no defense. He was executed by hanging on May 23, 1701.

Colonel Plug, the Riverboat Wrecker

Friedrich Fluger served in a New Hampshire regiment during the Civil War, and called himself "Colonel" after that, although the truth was that he never rose above the rank of Corporal. Fluger had been a farmer before the war, but he was not content with farming afterwards—he had glimpsed a different world as the tides of battle carried him through Virginia and the Carolinas, and he wanted to see more. So in 1866 he sold his eighty acres in Hillsborough County to an eager young couple from Shelburne, Vermont, and headed south.

Fluger started out with vague ideas of buying an abandoned plantation near Richmond or Charleston, and pretending to be the lord of the manor, but soon he discovered that a Yankee with a foreign-sounding voice would never be accepted by the people who counted there. Instead he drifted west, gave himself the title of "Colonel" when he reached Ohio, and dropped the name "Fluger" for good measure.

As Colonel Plotinus Plug, he traveled up and down the Ohio River on small steamboats—side-wheelers and stern-wheelers—meeting a wide assortment of gentlemen and ladies who welcomed him as long as he had cash. His new occupation was gambling. He had learned to play cards in the Army, and sometimes he did well at poker or faro, but on these riverboats he went up against some real cardsharks, who beat him more often than he beat them.

After two years of this, Colonel Plug was running out of money. He needed to find a new supply as soon as possible. He knew a lot of the people who worked on riverboats, and he was not greatly impressed by their courage or their intelligence. In fact, the Colonel figured that he could rob them without too much risk or effort.

Plug was right. He simply stood on the riverbank when a boat was due to come past, and shouted false warnings. More often than not, the man at the wheel would immediately change course without wondering who was warning him, and the boat would crash into big underwater rocks or other hidden obstacles, just as Colonel Plug had planned. Then the passengers and crew would swim ashore, expecting a long wet walk to the nearest town, only to find that the Colonel had set up a makeshift tent for them, with blankets and hot drinks. He didn't want anybody to suffer.

After watching his victims leave the area, Colonel Plug would row out to the wreck and search it quickly for valuables. He'd be long gone by the time anyone came along to salvage the riverboat, and with a little luck he could clear enough money to live comfortably and gamble for another month or two—even if he lost, as he frequently did.

Then came a fateful evening when the Colonel looked down at his cards and realized that he was bored—he held a pair of sevens and a pair of nines, but he didn't really care whether he won the hand or not. He was much more excited about the robbery he had planned for the next day. At midnight he excused himself from the poker game and took a long walk around the upper deck in the moonlight, wondering what it would be like to make robbery his full-time job.

"Only way to find out is to try it," he told himself.

The next day, when the riverboat stopped at Portsmouth, Ohio, the Colonel bought some tools that would fit in his suitcase, and carried them aboard. That night

he climbed down a steep ladder into the cargo hold, where he drilled some one-inch holes in the boat's wooden bottom. As the water poured in, passengers and crew leaped overboard and swam to shore, giving Plug just enough time to look for money, watches, and jewelry before the boat sank. Then he swam away to the opposite shore, pulling a little raft full of valuables behind him.

This plan succeeded several times, until Colonel Plug got careless. One day he left his suitcase open on the bed. Somebody noticed his tools and told the captain, who promptly locked the Colonel in an empty cabin with one small porthole. Plug had trouble breathing. Hours later the riverboat hit a sunken tree, rolling onto its side as it started to sink. People screamed and hollered, then jumped overboard and started swimming. Nobody heard Plug's frantic cries for help, or saw his hand reaching up through dark and muddy water, as though to clutch at air.

Billy the Kid

William H. Bonney was born in New York City on November 23, 1859. Little is known about his childhood, except that his mother took him to Santa Fe, New Mexico, when he was three, and he killed someone who had insulted her, in Silver City, when he was twelve. After that he evidently wandered around for several years, living and working on cattle ranches, learning a little Spanish, learning things about people, but above all learning how handy he was with guns. He had an extremely sharp eye, very fast reflexes, and a cool, fearless attitude towards matters of life and death. Thus he could hit anything that stood still, and almost anything that moved—a bear a mile away, birds flying up from the sagebrush, or anyone who tried to beat him to the draw. Shortly before his death at age twenty-one, Billy used to brag that he had killed twenty-one men, one for each year of his life. He wounded dozens of others in gunfights, but incredibly he was never hit himself, until his close friend and last enemy, Pat Garrett, shot him dead.

At that time, Pat had recently been elected Sheriff of Lincoln County, New Mexico. An unlikely lawman, he might have become an outlaw himself if certain things in his life had turned out differently. He had met Billy the Kid about three years earlier, before he started wearing a badge. They had taken to each other immediately, although they seemed like exact opposites. Pat was tall, thin-faced, soft-spoken, originally from Louisiana, a little slower than Billy to draw his gun, and a lot slower to actually pull the trigger. Billy was five foot eight inches tall, almost handsome, with a carefree smile and the gray eyes of a wolf. Walking down the street together in some dusty little town, Pat would be gazing at the grassy hills beyond, wondering if he might own a ranch there someday, while Billy would be staring down the men they passed, hoping that one or another had nerve enough to make trouble.

When Billy got hired to fight in the cattle wars of Lincoln County, at age eighteen, he urged Pat Garrett to come in with him, but Pat was just honest enough to say no. The leader of Billy's side, L. G. Murphy, was a businessman and rancher whose herds never seemed to get smaller, no matter how many head of cattle he sold. The leader of the opposing side, John Chisum, owned so many steers that he had never thought of counting them—until somebody tipped him off. Now Chisum was accusing Murphy of rustling his cattle in a big way, and Murphy was trying to pay him back quickly and cheaply, with lead instead of gold.

Billy, the fastest gun on either side, killed several of Chisum's cowboys and gradually assumed command of Murphy's gang of gunslingers and thieves. Later, when Chisum brought the law in on his side, Billy shot several members of the posse, including Sheriff Brady, whose job was taken over by Pat Garrett the following year. As more and more men on both sides were killed, news of this cattle war spread across the country, and the President of the United States sent a well-known general to make peace. Murphy and Chisum agreed to stop fighting, but some of Murphy's men did not. Led by Billy the Kid, they holed up in a remote canyon and continued rustling cattle on their own.

Billy had become a wanted criminal, and the reward for his capture, dead or alive, was steadily increasing. Deputy sheriffs and U.S. marshals went after him with larger and larger posses, but Billy always managed to avoid their traps or to shoot his way out. He had as many hideouts as a coyote has holes, and he became so quick and clever in his last year, dodging from one place to another, that some people doubted he would ever get caught.

Finally, on July 14, 1881, Pat Garrett stumbled into Billy's last hideout and shot him in the dark. He hung up his Sheriff's badge a few months later. When asked what he thought about Billy, Pat wrote something like an epitaph:

"The Kid had a lurking devil in him. It was a good-humored, jovial imp, or a cruel and blood-thirsty fiend, as circumstances prompted. Circumstances favored the worser angel, and the Kid fell."

Other Tales of Outlaws, Crooks, and Cheaters

Blackbeard the pirate, whose real name may have been Edward Teach or Tinch, was a folk character of his own making. Tall, hairy, outrageously dressed, he would stick lighted splinters in his hat and beard to frighten people, then go roaring into action with a cutlass in either hand. His apelike arms were so long that few enemies could touch him in a sword fight—he killed hundreds before being fatally shot in 1718. Stories about Blackbeard's returning ghost and buried treasure are still told in his favorite haunts, the outer banks of North Carolina.

José Gaspar was a Spanish naval officer entrusted to carry some of the crown jewels in his ship. Overcome by temptation, he stole them and embarked upon a new life of crime, calling himself "King of the Pirates." Gaspar specialized in stealing women as well as gold and jewels. He established his base of operations on an island near Tampa, Florida, and preyed on the shipping of the Caribbean and the Gulf of Mexico for years, until an American warship blew him out of the water in 1821.

Moll Diamond grew up in Marblehead, Massachusetts, within sight of the sea. For more than fifty years she predicted which ships would return safely to port, and she was usually right. At first people accused her of cheating in some way, though they could never explain just how, and Moll was insulted. Later they said she was a witch, but Moll didn't mind, because she believed her father, John, to be a wizard.

Belle Starr, the gorgeous daughter of a bank robber named Henry Starr, took over her father's gang and enlarged it after he died. From the 1870s to the 1880s she ran wild in the territory that later became Oklahoma, earning the title "Queen of the Bandits" from the *Police Gazette*. Ambushed and killed on her forty-third birthday, Belle was buried beneath this inscription:

> *Shed not for her the bitter tear,*
> *Nor give thy heart to vain regret—*
> *'Tis but the casket that lies here,*
> *The gem that fills it sparkles yet.*

Dowsabel Casselman met two disturbing strangers at the inn her parents kept near Somerset, Pennsylvania. The first was young and handsome, the second was old and wrinkled, but both wore black cloaks and black hats with golden eagle feathers in them. Gradually Dowsabel realized that the two men were ghosts of the same person, David Lewis, a smooth-talking thief who had been killed by a sheriff's posse years earlier. The young ghost romanced her, while the old one involved her in a complicated scheme to bring him back to life. In the end they both disappeared unsatisfied.

Timothy Dexter, born in New England in 1747, had the Midas touch. From the time he entered business to the day he died, Dexter made a profit from almost all of his investments, no matter how far-fetched they might be. He sold coal in the South, ice in the North, harness to people who had no mules, and mules to people who had no wagons. If cars had been invented then, he could have sold them in places without roads. Dexter was more generous than selfish, however. He kept enough of his wealth to live comfortably, in the style of "Lord Dexter," but he gave away the rest.

Sam Slick was typical of the Yankee peddlers who traveled around America during the nineteenth century, starting in New England, later following the frontier as it moved westward. Sam could sell almost anything to almost anybody, not because they needed it but because he'd talk them into believing they did—just long enough for him to take their money and move on. On rare occasions a sly backwoodsman would attempt to outwit him, asking for some nonsensical item such as a goose-yoke or a left-handed knife, but the city slicker usually had the last laugh.

Other folk characters who usually laughed last include Peck's Bad Boy and Little Audrey. Like other rambunctious children in earlier folk tales, the Bad Boy wasn't really bad, of course; if he did something naughty, this was just his way of calling attention to the frauds or shenanigans of grown-ups. Little Audrey was more of a spectator, characteristically finding humor by twisting the misdeeds or misfortunes of adults. If somebody said their house had been robbed, for example, Little Audrey just laughed and laughed, because she knew their house never owned anything.

Butch Cassidy, the Sundance Kid, the Fiddleback Kid, the Tall Texan, Poker John—a host of gunmen are characters in numerous folk tales about the Wild West. Extremely quick and accurate with rifles or pistols, they often had hair-trigger tempers that led to eruptions of violence. Sometimes they killed one another, but other times they banded together, in groups such as the Wild Bunch and the Hole-in-the-Wall Gang, supporting themselves by rustling cattle and robbing banks or trains. Their hideouts were like fortresses, bristling with guns.

The most dangerous of all the Western gunslingers was Harvey Logan, an orphan who became leader of a juvenile gang including his younger brothers and cousins. Calling himself "Kid Curry," he stole his first Colt .44 when he was only twelve and fired his last shot to kill himself in 1903—old, wounded, and surrounded by heavily armed Pinkerton detectives. In between he gunned down dozens of bank guards and lawmen, and more than a few outlaws who could not beat him to the draw.

For additional tales, see Robert Howard's *This Is the West,* Horace Beck's *The Folklore of Maine,* and Eric Partridge's *Pirates, Highwaymen and Adventurers,* among other sources.

HEROINES AND HEROES

Eliza Crossing the Ice

Eliza Harris, daughter and granddaughter of slaves, lived on a tobacco plantation near Elizabethtown, Kentucky, in the 1840s. Eliza's granny used to tell her the town was named after her, but as Eliza grew older and wiser she realized that nothing would be named after her, not even her own children, unless she made it happen. Working in the fields from sunup to sundown, she had plenty of time to think. At age eighteen, when she learned she was going to have a baby, Eliza decided her child must not be born in slavery—she would run away some dark night soon.

On her first attempt, Eliza got more than a mile from the plantation before one of the white overseers tracked her down on horseback. The dogs cornered her against a thicket of hawthorns and slobbered on her bare legs, because they had been trained not to bite. The overseer said nothing to Eliza. He simply threw a burlap sack over her head, tied it with twine, and trotted her back to the slave cabins like a turkey on a leash. Eliza wasn't hurt physically, but she ached with anger and humiliation.

After two more attempts to escape under cover of darkness, Eliza was brought before the chief overseer, a burly red-haired man who had no time for sympathy or cruelty. The plantation was simply a business to him, and he was determined to do a good job of running it for his absentee masters.

"You might lose your baby if you run away again," he told her matter-of-factly. "I'm going to have you locked up at night."

Eliza remained silent. Several other slaves who worked the fields were locked in chains each night because they had tried to escape. Eliza learned from their experiences.

"By day those overseers be so busy bossin' everyone," an older woman advised her. "Best you try then."

Younger runaways gave Eliza similar advice, though most were discouraged about trying again themselves.

"Don't know where to go if I do get loose," a man said. "Nobody around these parts going to help."

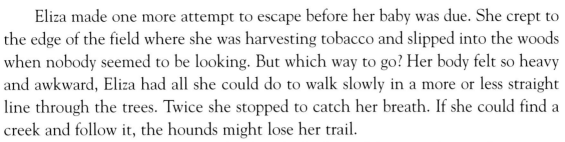

Eliza made one more attempt to escape before her baby was due. She crept to the edge of the field where she was harvesting tobacco and slipped into the woods when nobody seemed to be looking. But which way to go? Her body felt so heavy and awkward, Eliza had all she could do to walk slowly in a more or less straight line through the trees. Twice she stopped to catch her breath. If she could find a creek and follow it, the hounds might lose her trail.

Beyond the sheltering woods, she climbed a rail fence and started across an open field of hay, with cows grazing in the distance. Moments later, she heard horses galloping. Two of the Harris overseers caught up with her, one on each side, and held her between them with ropes. Eliza fell to the ground moaning. When they pulled her upright again, she burst into tears.

"Spare my baby," she begged, before she fainted.

Late that night Eliza regained consciousness, chained to a bed, in great pain. She tossed and turned. Someone wiped her hot forehead with a damp cloth. Women's voices gently comforted her. She fainted again. Pain came and went. The next morning, she awoke to greet her own child—a girl, healthy and hungry and loud.

"What you goin' to name her?" a woman asked.

"*Freedom!*" cried Eliza, still excited and confused. Later the chief overseer told her this name was not acceptable, so she chose Frieda as a substitute, or rather she pretended to—in her own mind and in her heart, the little girl's name was Freedom from that very first moment of maternal pride.

With her baby to nurse, in addition to working all day in the fields, Eliza had little time to think about escaping. The overseers relaxed their vigilance and allowed her to sleep in her own bed, without chains. As the months passed, however, her daughter Freedom grew bigger and stronger and more intelligent. Again Eliza began to wonder how she could make freedom a reality for both of them.

When little Freedom was almost two years old, several of the male slaves tried to escape together. They stole a wagon and traveled as fast as they could down the rutted country roads that led to Louisville. From there they hoped to find their way to the Northern states where slavery had been abolished. But having no real plans and no help, they were soon caught and brought back in that same wagon, tied hand and foot. They were whipped, then chained to posts in the yard.

A white-haired slave named Israel, who knew much of the Bible by heart, tried to comfort these miserable men spiritually. Listening to him speak, Eliza too was comforted. But the comfort she felt did not last long. Reassurance swept through her like the heat of righteousness. It wasn't wrong to seek freedom, again and again—it was something she ought to do, she would do!

Eliza kept on asking questions, piecing together her knowledge of her surroundings. The Harris plantation was about twenty miles south of Kentucky's border with Ohio—a state that no longer permitted slavery—but there were obstacles along the way, including other plantations with overseers and hounds. Thick woods and hills, some of them cut by gullies and streams, separated these properties from one another. Finally there was the Ohio River, deep and swift, where several runaways were known to have drowned. The shortest route to the river, folks said, was to follow Otter Creek due north, as it flowed through the woods between farms. However, this route had been tried so many times that the overseers always looked there first.

"Best try a different way," someone suggested.

And how to get across the river when she reached it? That was another problem, but Eliza wasn't going to hold back. She'd find a boat, she'd swim, she'd do whatever she had to do.

Then someone said the river might freeze, come January or February. This had happened two years before, and some folks had escaped to Ohio across the ice! Eliza felt hope rising strongly within her.

"*This time we're going to make it,*" she assured Freedom, who smiled up at her trustingly.

November, December, Christmas—Eliza waited impatiently for the coldest weather. Most slaves were kept indoors, doing repairs and making burlap sacks for the next season, but a few of the men rode wagons to Louisville with the overseers and loaded tobacco onto flatboats.

"River frozen yet?" Eliza would ask them.

"Not yet."

"Not yet."

"A little bit."

"A little bit more."

On the first day of February, just before work stopped for the noon meal, Eliza hid young Freedom under her long cloak and walked out of the barn. Passing the main house unobserved, she entered the woods beyond it, not heading north toward Otter Creek but west instead.

"*Here we go, Freedom*," she murmured.

Eliza walked several miles until she came to a different creek, which was frozen. There she turned north, using the shadows of trees to guide her, as she had been taught by one of the other slaves. Stumbling, plunging through the thin ice sometimes, Eliza wearily followed the narrow creek more than thirty miles, stopping only to care for her little girl. Day after day, she felt no weariness, no hunger, no cold. In fact the weather was surprisingly warm.

At sunrise on the fourth day, Eliza came out of the woods on a high bluff. There was the river below her—not frozen solid, but moving in the middle—broken up into flat slabs of ice bigger than barn doors, separated by dark channels of water. Could she get across?

"*We're not stopping now*," Eliza thought.

Hounds howled in the distance. Eliza didn't look back. She held Freedom tight and slid down the slippery hill to the river's edge. Hounds were howling louder now. Eliza ran out onto the ice, which felt solid at first. Closer to the middle, though, where the ice had broken up into big pieces, she could see that the whole mass was moving slowly downstream. It was beautiful, but frightening.

Coming to the first narrow gap in the ice, Eliza stepped across to one of the huge floating slabs, maybe twenty feet wide. It tilted slightly under her weight, but it still felt solid. At the far edge, there was another gap two or three feet wide. Eliza ran, leaped, and made it. She slipped on the next slab, fell, but got up and went on to the next gap. Leaped. Then another gap, wider. Then another.

"*We can do it*," Eliza thought, holding Freedom high as she ran, and leaped, and ran on. The more she did it, the easier it seemed.

Behind her the overseers were shouting in frustration, but the dogs had given up already, and Eliza continued her crossing with amazing grace.

Barbara Frietchie Waves the Flag

Wild rumors flew among the peaceful residents of Frederick, Maryland, in September, 1862. The Civil War was about to engulf them! That legendary Southern general, Robert E. Lee, had outwitted his enemies again! Confederate troops were crossing the Potomac River at White's Ford, twenty-three miles away, and heading north. How many? Hundreds, maybe thousands! Why were they coming? Nobody knew for sure. Maryland was officially a border state, neither a member of the Confederacy nor part of the Union, but many people believed in one side or the other. As Lee's soldiers advanced, with Stonewall Jackson in the lead, Northern sympathizers pictured unruly hordes of ruffians descending upon them. Southern sympathizers envisioned an army of liberation, and perhaps a quick end to this bloody war. What they actually saw when the Confederates entered Frederick was a steady stream of tired, mostly barefoot young men with the hazy light of survival in their eyes.

Lee's strategy was essentially simple. He didn't have enough soldiers or supplies to win a long war. But if he could strike fear and panic into the hearts of Union leaders, especially the politicians and the generals, they might settle for peace. That would be as good as a decisive battle, and much less costly. Thus he threatened the jittery city of Washington from time to time, and he launched daring raids as far north as Maryland and Pennsylvania, beyond which the bountiful states of the North lay mostly open and defenseless.

From Lee's viewpoint, the little town of Frederick was merely a stopping point

on one of these raids. For his men, however, the stop was a great relief.
They had been moving—most of them on foot—for several weeks.
Many lacked shoes and clean uniforms. All of them were hungry—
their main source of food had been green corn, picked hastily in
the fields of Virginia and eaten raw as they struggled to keep up with
their leaders. Only the hope of finishing the war with honor had kept
them going.

Walking wearily into Frederick, they saw quiet streets and comfortable homes
untouched by war. They saw stores full of food and clothing. They saw townspeople looking out of windows and standing on the sidewalks—some smiling and
waving Confederate flags at them, others frowning as they displayed the Union's
stars and stripes.

Barbara Frietchie, age 96, had a different kind of banner hanging in her attic
window. Born in 1766, she had been given one of the first American flags at the
end of the Revolutionary War, and she proudly showed it now: red and white
stripes, and a blue field with thirteen white stars in a circle, one for each of the
original colonies. Virginia and several of the other Southern states had been
among those early colonies—today she hoped the sight of this flag might help to
remind Southerners of the parts their own grandparents had played in creating a
new nation.

Passing her house, some of the young Confederate soldiers were yelling and
firing their outdated muskets. As Mrs. Frietchie leaned from her window to look
at them, a musket ball flew past her ear, bouncing off the attic ceiling and hitting
the opposite wall. Another hit her precious old flag! Barbara Frietchie was
enraged.

"You there, you rebels!" she called down to the excited men. "How dare you
fire at the flag of your country? Shoot me if you have to, but not your flag!"

"That there ain't my flag, lady," one of the soldiers shouted back at her.
"Never seen it before—don't know as I'd care to see it again!" There was more
yelling, gunfire, laughter.

Barbara Frietchie's hands trembled as she took her flag inside and closed the
window. She wept, and some of her tears fell on the faded cloth. "Whatever will
become of our dear country?" she said to herself. She went slowly downstairs. The
next morning she told the story to anyone who would listen.

Stonewall Jackson heard about it a few days later. He fully intended to ride
over to Mrs. Frietchie's house and apologize before leaving town—for true or false,
this was a blemish on the honor of the army which he led. But then he learned
that Union troops were coming in his direction at last, and he forgot about Mrs.
Frietchie's flag as he rode towards the village of Antietam to do battle.

Molly Pitcher in the Revolution

Herman Hays and Mary Ludwig were an odd-looking couple. She was a big, strong Pennsylvania German woman, comely and wise, who had turned away one suitor after another before Herman came along. He was short, nearly bald, at least ten years older than Mary, but sparkling and witty. He amused her the first time they met, at her uncle's blacksmith shop in Schwenksville, when he offered to buy some old muskets on account.

"On account of what?" Mary asked.

"On account of George Washington needs guns to fight the British redcoats, and he has very little money at the moment," Herman replied, with his most winning smile.

"That's not funny," Mary said, but she returned his smile in spite of herself. "Do you work for General Washington?" she continued.

"Not exactly," Herman admitted. "Let's just say I represent his interests, whenever he allows me to do so."

"And he needs these guns my uncle has been repairing?"

"Precisely," Herman said.

He returned in July with a small amount of cash and a scribbled note supposedly from the General. Mary was skeptical. Her uncle, however, would do anything he could to help "The Father of His Country," as Washington was known among the Germans of Pennsylvania.

"Let Herman take the guns," Mary suggested, "but let me go with him to make sure he delivers them to Washington's army."

It was a long, slow wagon ride through eastern Pennsylvania and across New Jersey to Washington's encampment near Monmouth. Herman told Mary the story of his life—from his birth in a prison in Liverpool, England, through his service as gunner's mate on a British warship, to his arrival in America, penniless and free, just three years ago. Mary had never heard anything half as exciting.

"And every word of it true, or nearly so," he told her with his charming smile.

"Oh Herman, you silly man," said Mary. But he delighted her, and truth to tell, she delighted him as well. By the time they reached the Delaware River they were in love, and as they passed through Trenton they got married.

The next day, crossing the sun-baked flatlands of New Jersey, they heard the thunderous sounds of cannon fire in the distance.

"Fifteen pounders," said Herman. "That'll be the British, blowing holes in our lads from a safe distance."

"Don't the Americans have cannons too?" Mary asked anxiously.

"Smaller ones," Herman replied, "and not much ammunition, so they don't shoot until the redcoats are almost on top of them."

He urged the horses forward, while Mary clung to him. Their wagon raced through the scrub pines into a large clearing, where blue-coated American soldiers formed a thin defensive line. Others lay wounded on the ground. Masses of British redcoats were advancing towards them.

Then Herman saw some Americans struggling with a large cannon they had captured from the British. He quickly hitched his horses to the big gun, swung it around, and showed the untrained young soldiers how to clean it and load a cannonball weighing fifteen pounds.

"Ready—Aim—Fire!" Herman shouted. "Again! Ready—Aim—Fire!"

With Herman in charge the cannon fired rapidly and accurately at the approaching British troops. Meanwhile, Mary found a pitcher somewhere, and carried water from a nearby spring to exhausted soldiers. Suddenly a troop of redcoated cavalry attacked them, swinging sabers and shooting pistols. Mary cried out, as Herman fell beneath their hooves. One after another the Americans were hit. The captured cannon was silent.

"Molly, Molly Pitcher, bring us water," a voice cried weakly, but Mary had no time to be merciful now. She loaded the heavy cannon as she had seen Herman do it, and fired into the midst of the charging redcoats. Some were killed or wounded, others ran away. A few Americans ran after them.

"You've won this battle for us, Molly Pitcher," an American officer shouted.

But Mary thought only of finding Herman's body, loading it into the wagon, and driving back to Schwenksville with her grief.

Finding a Way to the Northwest

Meriwether Lewis and William Clark set forth in 1804 to explore a new territory called "Louisiana," which the United States had recently purchased from France. This territory was much larger than the state of Louisiana as we know it today. Starting at the Mississippi River, it extended westward about two thousand miles, taking in the vast plains of the Midwest, then the Rockies and other high mountains, range after range. Lewis and Clark were given the job of finding a route across "Upper Louisiana"—preferably a route that settlers could follow—all the way to the Pacific Ocean.

The two men had explored parts of this territory before. They knew that a very long river, the Missouri, flows through it from the west. Therefore they decided to start at St. Louis, where the Missouri joins the Mississippi River like a sideways T, and follow the Missouri back to its western source. If they were lucky, it might lead them through the mountains to the Pacific coast, somewhere between California and Canada.

Starting with forty-five men and women in three boats, Lewis and Clark followed the wide, smooth river, west and then north. Rowing against the current, they went slowly through what is now Missouri, Kansas, Nebraska, and the Dakotas. At first the land was flat or gently rolling, the fish and game were abundant, and the native people were hospitable. The explorers spent the winter of 1804–5 camping in North Dakota with Mandan Indians, who helped them build light and portable canoes to replace their clumsy wooden boats.

When spring came, Lewis and Clark continued following the Missouri almost to the Canadian border, entering a maze of lakes and rivers that seemed to flow in all directions. They hoped one of these rivers would be the next stretch of the Missouri, taking them further west, but they couldn't tell which one. Then a young Shoshone woman named Sacajawea helped them. Although she was timid and spoke no English yet, Sacajawea communicated her remarkable grasp of geography through her husband, Charbonneau, an interpreter with the expedition.

"Sacajawea say, 'No go this way,'" he reported. "'Go other way.'"

"But so many of these rivers look alike," Lewis replied. "How can she be sure?"

Charbonneau spoke to his wife, who dipped her fingers into the water.

"She say, 'Feel water, this way colder, river come from western mountains,'" he explained.

"Hard to believe," Lewis murmured, "all of this water feels the same to me."

But he was eager to move on, and so was Clark. After a brief conference, they decided to take Sacajawea's advice. Saying nothing more, she trailed her fingers in the chilly water as they canoed along, leaving the lake that is called "Sakakawea" today.

Crossing North Dakota, they came to the unexplored hills of Montana, where the going was much more difficult. Often the canoes and baggage had to be carried around waterfalls and through rapids. There was no easy path beside the river. Members of the expedition became weary, hungry, ill. Ferocious wolves and grizzly bears frightened them. Ahead, steeper and steeper hills gave way to mountain ranges, peaks crowned with snow. Knowing they had to get through those mountains before winter, the explorers pushed onward.

The river was narrower and rougher now, a tumult of white water rushing down between rocky walls. Canoes had become useless, yet the explorers still carried them, hoping to find smoother passages. Day after day they climbed higher. Finally they came to the headwaters of the Missouri, the place where it actually begins, and realized that this river is not a road to the ocean after all—the western mountains towered thousands of feet above them. How could they go further?

Sacajawea saved them, not with map or compass but by sensing natural things—air on her cheek, slight changes in vegetation, patterns of shadow and light. Striding along, she discovered a way between the snow-capped mountains—a pass that crosses the highest ridge in the country, the Continental Divide, at seven thousand feet. From there the route to the Pacific was still difficult, down through the hills of Idaho and Oregon to the coast, but Lewis and Clark found other rivers to follow. Now they didn't need Sacajawea to guide them. In their excitement, she was left behind and almost forgotten.

The Unsinkable Mrs. Brown

Like other great men and women, Molly Brown appeared when she was needed to perform heroic deeds. Unlike most of them, however, she did not disappear afterwards. Loud, somewhat flashy, and always full of fun, Mrs. Brown lived proudly in the limelight for twenty years, telling and retelling the story of how a courageous American female had rescued passengers from a damaged ocean liner, *Titanic*, as it was sinking.

Mrs. Brown's opportunity for heroism came when she was already middle-aged. Traveling to Europe early in 1912 without her busy husband, she had met dozens of fascinating people in London and Paris, and she had purchased some wonderfully bizarre hats and outlandish dresses. Now it was April, time for her long journey home to Colorado. With seven trunks packed and labeled, Mrs. Brown took a train to Cherbourg, France. Awaiting her at dockside was the *Titanic*, an enormous new ship designed to be fast and unsinkable, whose destination was New York. Mrs. Brown climbed the gangplank slowly, huffing and puffing, for the European restaurants and pastry shops had added more weight to her already plump figure. She promised herself to walk at least a mile a day during the trip.

But first, being Molly Brown, she wanted people to know who she was and what she was about. "People" meant absolutely everybody, passengers and crew—

she simply had to get their attention and win them over. She did this in a variety of ways, according to her own moods. Once or twice she sang at the afternoon concerts, her deep voice just a little louder than anyone else's. When she was bubbling over with mischief, she'd lead children on madcap races from one end of the ship to the other. And when she was feeling really feisty, she would take her pearl-handled Colt .45 revolver to the stern of the ship and start shooting at fresh oranges or grapefruits tossed high out over the waves. Seagulls would follow the swift *Titanic* for hours, puzzled by the bullet-punctured fruit that trailed behind it.

At the end of each day aboard ship, Mrs. Brown would change into a flamboyant gown, purple with diamonds or green with rubies, and do something original to her hair. Then she'd entertain her fellow passengers at the largest table in the dining salon. She'd tell stories about her early life as Margaret Tobin back East, about meeting her future husband out West, about people in Denver and the mining towns, about looking for lead and finding gold—stories so vivid and funny that even the stuffiest listeners were amused.

After dinner, Mrs. Brown would change her clothes again to go walking around the deck. Because the evenings were cold, she'd start with extra-heavy woolen underwear, silk bloomers, two jersey petticoats. Then she'd add an ankle-length cashmere dress, golf stockings, high calfskin boots, a man's cap tied with a scarf, and a muff of Russian sable—tucking her Colt .45 inside it, just in case. Over all of this, she'd put on a chinchilla opera cloak that had cost her husband $60,000 in 1910. Wearing so much, she couldn't walk very briskly, but she kept at it until she had done a mile or more.

Molly Brown and other passengers were still walking and talking one evening when the *Titanic* ran into something—an iceberg, they were told later—with a horrendous crash. People screamed, bells rang, whistles blew, lights came on all over the ship, and there was total confusion among passengers and crew. The captain's voice could be heard, urging everyone to stay calm, but soon the ship was settling lower in the water, obviously sinking, and people knew it. The captain's voice faded away. Other voices were shouting orders that nobody seemed to follow.

That's when Molly Brown took charge, getting the lifeboats lowered and the passengers into them, waving her .45 to back up her loud commands. Women and children went first, except Mrs. Brown—she refused to leave the sinking *Titanic* until it was almost too late. Then she climbed awkwardly down into the last lifeboat, found a seat, gave most of her warm clothing to others who were thinly dressed. After looking back once, fixing that terrible scene in her memory, she kept the tired men rowing mile after mile with prayers, songs, threats, promises—whatever it took to overcome the darkness and the sea.

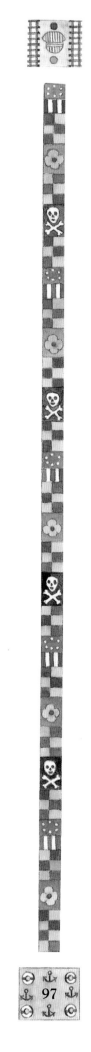

Texas Ranger

Although he grew up on a Florida plantation surrounded by wealth, Jefferson Davis Milton quit school in 1877, when he was fifteen, to work in a grocery store. A year later he left home for good, taking only his favorite horse, his Winchester rifle, and a few clothes. Jeff's father, the Governor of Florida at the time, decided to send a man after him—not to bring him back, for that could only make things worse, but just to keep an eye on him. For this task Governor Milton selected a private detective, William Hardaway, who was called "Hardway Bill" because he seldom did things the easy way unless he had to.

Hardway Bill sent telegrams out in all directions to railroad stations, big-city police, and army posts. He soon picked up Jeff Milton's trail in the Florida panhandle, leapfrogged ahead of him by train, and sat waiting in a light wagon as the young man crossed the Pearl River into Louisiana. Never one to beat around the bush, Hardway Bill introduced himself and explained what he was doing.

"And where might you be headed?" he inquired.

"South Texas, to stay with my uncle," Jeff replied pleasantly. "Are you going to follow me the whole way?"

"I reckon that's what the Governor hired me for," said Hardway Bill. "You go ahead, and I'll stay behind you a ways, so you won't be embarrassed."

That's how they started out, but the arrangement seemed foolish to both of them after a while, so Jeff ended up riding in the wagon with Hardway Bill while his horse trotted along behind. It took them four weeks to find the uncle's ranch, all the way down on the Rio Grande near Laredo, and by then the two of them were easy companions, if not exactly friends.

Jeff spent the next two years punching cows and herding wild horses, while Hardway Bill kept him company, still acting under orders from Governor Milton. When he reached the age of eighteen, Jeff tried to end this arrangement, but Hardway Bill was stubborn and the Governor was still willing to pay. A few weeks later, Jeff had a bright idea.

"I'm going to join the Texas Rangers," he said. "See if you can follow me then."

"That's a mighty tough outfit," Hardway Bill responded. "I doubt if they'd let you in. Besides, you got to be twenty-one to join up."

Hardway Bill knew this because he had been thinking about joining the Rangers himself, if and when his job as paid companion petered out, but he figured Jeff would find out for himself. Jeff fooled Bill, however, by growing a thin mustache and adding three years to his true age. The Rangers signed him up, and Jeff went off to the Ranger station at Hackberry Springs in July, 1880, for training. Hardway Bill didn't go along.

Despite the intense heat, Jeff took to the Ranger's life very easily. He learned to shoot better, to ride faster, to think for himself in any situation, and above all to uphold the law. At first he was assigned to a company of more experienced Rangers, patrolling the dangerous new towns that were springing up across the Texas plains as two railroad lines were being built. Jeff handled himself so well that he was soon promoted and sent alone to one of those towns, whose sheriff had telegraphed the Rangers for help with a riot of construction workers. When Jeff stepped down from the train, this sheriff was astonished.

"There's only one of you?" he asked.

"There's only one riot, isn't there?" Jeff replied.

Jeff unloaded his horse from a boxcar, rode slowly through the angry mob, and arrested several troublemakers without firing a shot. The rest of the workers went quietly back to their camp, and Jeff got his next assignment by telegram from Ranger headquarters. A masked bandit, driving a wagon, had held up the bank in Laredo and was last seen racing north. Jeff changed horses twice, intercepted the bandit on a road leading to San Antonio, and found that it was his old watchdog, Hardway Bill.

"Why?" he asked bluntly.

"Well, after your father quit paying me, Jeff, I ran out of money, and—"

"For Pete's sake, Bill, you could have borrowed some from me."

"I knew I could," said Hardway Bill, with the saddest smile, "but that would have been too easy."

Elfrego Baca, the Fearless Deputy

Back in the days when the Wild West was truly wild, deputy sheriffs could be tall, short, fat, skinny, young, or sometimes old. Elfrego Baca, for instance, was young, short, and skinny, nothing much to look at. He kept his deputy's badge polished, however, and his Colt revolvers too, with ammunition belts crossed low on his hips, and holsters tied down like a gunfighter's. What could anyone tell from that? Elfrego might be a tough little *hombre*, ready to enforce the law at any cost, or maybe he just wanted people to think so.

After two years of service, Elfrego had a problem: there was very little excitement in the town of Frisco, New Mexico, where he worked. His elderly boss, the sheriff, patrolled the streets at night and made any arrests that were necessary. Elfrego was stuck with the boring jobs—guarding prisoners and fetching their meals, cleaning out cells, plus doing the paperwork because his boss supposedly couldn't read or write.

Late one Saturday afternoon in March of 1884, Elfrego finished writing a report, closed the sheriff's large rolltop desk, and strolled down the main street of the town to see what was happening. Very little, as usual. Passing the saloon where his boss was enjoying some liquid refreshment, Elfrego continued along the wooden sidewalk to the livery stable. He told the man who ran it that he would need to hire an extra horse on Monday.

"Where you going, Deputy?"

"Sheriff's sending me over to *Pasiente,* to deliver a prisoner for trial next week."

Pasiente, slang for El Paso, was just a few miles away from Frisco, and that was where Federal judges held court for southern New Mexico as well as the northwest corner of Texas. Elfrego's prisoner, a Texan, had been in and out of the Frisco jail a dozen times before.

"What's he done this time?" asked the stable owner. "Drunk and disorderly again?"

"No, worse than that," said Elfrego. "He chased a girl into the *barrio* last night. Hurt her pretty bad. Then he shot her little brother."

"Nobody told me," the man said.

Elfrego wasn't surprised. Even in a small town like Frisco, the Mexican neighborhood was a distinct and separate world that most of the other residents didn't know much about.

Back in the office, with nothing to do, Elfrego looked at the latest stack of WANTED posters. Some pretty bad characters, and some pretty big rewards being offered, but nothing connected with the town of Frisco. Just to keep his mind sharp, however, Elfrego made a list of names, and tried to memorize the faces that went with them.

"Hey, jailer," a voice growled from the row of cells behind him. Elfrego turned. It was the troublemaking Texan he had to take to El Paso next week.

"So you're awake," Elfrego said. "What can I do for you?"

"Steak, fried eggs, and plenty of coffee," said the cowboy, whose name was Frank Magee. "And be quick about it—I'm hungry enough to eat the front half of a steer, horns and all."

"I'll bring you some food as soon as the sheriff gets back," said Elfrego.

Magee started cursing. Elfrego ignored him. He had no other prisoners to guard today, but now that this fellow was up, he didn't want to leave him alone, even in the locked jail.

"You can't keep me here like this," Magee shouted. "I'm an American citizen, and I know my rights."

"You'll go before the judge in El Paso on Monday or Tuesday," Elfrego replied. "Until then you're staying right here—"

"When I get my hands on you," Magee was roaring, "I'll—"

"Partly for your own protection," Elfrego continued. "A few people in this town would like to have words with you."

"People or Mexicans?" Magee sneered. "There's a big difference where I come from."

"But maybe not such a big difference where you're going," Elfrego said under his breath.

"What's that?" cried Magee, rattling the barred door of his cell. "Why you ornery little—"

At this moment the sheriff walked in, caught the tone of the conversation, belched, and sat down at his desk.

"Go get some food for the prisoner," he told Elfrego, tossing him a silver dollar.

"And don't forget my coffee," Magee shouted after him.

Outside, Elfrego breathed deeply and leaned against the wall of the jail for a moment. It would be wrong to hit a prisoner, of course, but still—he took another deep breath and looked around.

Sunset had turned the sky blood-red between old adobe buildings. Though Frisco didn't have much to offer, it seemed a lot better than nothing on a Saturday night. The street was busy now with townspeople and cowboys from the nearby ranches and other folks looking for some kind of fun. As he walked towards the saloon to get a tray of food for the prisoner, Elfrego recognized most of the people passing. No, here were some strangers hitching their horses in front of the saloon. Cowboys. Ten or twelve of them. Texans, by the way they talked.

One of them pulled a shotgun out of a saddlebag, and Elfrego instantly reached for his pistols—but a moment later the man put the weapon away and went into the saloon with his companions. Elfrego relaxed, followed the strangers inside, and observed them quietly as he waited for his order to be filled. A dozen big men, roughly dressed, each wearing one or two guns. Talking loud and drinking a lot. Apparently they had money. Suddenly

one of them turned towards Elfrego—this man looked like Frank Magee! Maybe a brother or a cousin of the prisoner—maybe the Texans were going to try a jail-break! Elfrego quickly paid for the food and hurried out.

He found the sheriff asleep in a chair. Magee, the prisoner, was lying on his bunk. Elfrego set the tray down on a table and unlocked the cell. Magee leaped up, grabbed Elfrego, overpowered him, and snatched one of his pistols, firing a wild shot into the floor. This awakened the sheriff, who reached under his coat for a gun as Magee fired again and killed him.

"Put your other pistol on the table there, or you're a dead man," Magee shouted at Elfrego.

The young deputy did as he was told. Then Magee leaned forward to pick up the pistol, and Elfrego hit him in the face with a full pot of hot coffee. Magee fell to his knees, screaming. Elfrego took both pistols away and put handcuffs on him, but Magee was too heavy to drag back into the cell, so the deputy used another pair of cuffs to fasten the prisoner's arm to a leg of the sheriff's massive desk. Magee, moaning with pain, asked for water. Elfrego pushed a bucket towards him with the handle of a broom.

"Use what's left in that," said Elfrego. His heart was beating like an Apache drum, but he knew what he had to do—lock the door, secure the windows, and start loading the extra guns that the sheriff had stored in a closet.

"You're wasting your time," Magee snarled. "The front of this jail is going to blow wide open an hour from now. And you, *chiquito*, you're going to meet your Maker about five minutes after that!"

Elfrego didn't answer. He used tables and chairs to barricade the windows and the door as best he could, and placed the loaded guns where he could reach them in a hurry. Meanwhile, Magee was crouching under the heavy desk, as close to the floor as possible.

BAM! The front door exploded into splinters of wood and scraps of metal. Elfrego felt something cut his cheek. Smoke filled the room, and bullets flew through the shattered doorway. Masked figures could be seen dimly in the street, guns blazing.

"I'm going to chase your friends away," Elfrego told Magee.

"Fat chance," Magee responded.

Elfrego cleared the street with rapid fire from two Winchester carbines, one after the other. Men shouted and scattered. Then he stood in the doorway with a third Winchester, picking off the outlaws as they showed themselves to shoot at him. Gradually their guns were silenced. Elfrego was nicked a couple of times, but not seriously hurt. After it was all over, he walked outside and said a little prayer of thanks.

Years later, when he was studying to be a lawyer, Elfrego was asked about his famous gunfight back in Frisco.

"I heard it was eighty to one against you," the man said. "I heard you killed more than half of them before they gave up."

"There were only twelve to start with," Elfrego replied, "and I'd say I wounded three, maybe four, but I didn't kill anybody. You know how those Texans love to exaggerate."

Van Wempel's Goose

It was the week after Christmas, 1899, and the island of Manhattan lay covered by a sparkling crust of snow which had just begun to freeze. Henry Van Wempel, hurrying home to his new wife, Louisa, laughed like a schoolboy as he skidded and slid on the icy pavement. Other houses looked inviting, but they could not compare to his! Candles in the front windows, holly wreath on the door, sand where the steps might be slippery—everything just right. Louisa!

He rushed inside to embrace her—blonde, a little stout in her build, very pretty, smiling at him—no, not smiling this time. Frowning, it seemed.

"What's the matter, my darling?" he cried, still cheerful.

"Tomorrow night is New Year's Eve," she replied, looking at him oddly.

"Indeed it is, my precious."

"And tonight you were supposed to bring me a goose."

"Goose?" he repeated. "Goose for what?"

"Goose for New Year's dinner, of course."

"But in my family, Louisa, we've always had turkey and ham."

"In my family we've always had goose," she responded, as if that settled the matter.

And so it did, as far as Van Wempel was concerned, for he adored Louisa. They had been married less than a year, and he found great pleasure in doing things to please her. A goose for New Year's dinner? Why not! He vaguely remembered a farmers' market on Staten Island, with live white geese for sale.

"I know just the place to get one," he murmured, but Louisa scarcely heard him, for now she was busy putting supper on the table—fat sausages, mashed potatoes and gravy, carrots cooked with their tops on—one of his favorite meals. He sat down to eat and she hovered a moment before joining him. She was just as eager to please her new husband as he was to please her.

"Delicious!" he exclaimed, and they both smiled.

The next day Van Wempel closed his waterfront office early, wished his clerks a Happy New Year, and rode the trolley to the tip of Manhattan where he could catch a ferryboat across the harbor to Staten Island. A chilly wind made the water choppy, but Van Wempel found the weather invigorating. He hadn't taken this ride in years, so he was one of the few passengers who stood outside despite the cold, seeing the Statue of Liberty and other sights as though for the first time. How wonderful! Just before the ferry docked, Van Wempel glanced back at the spires and towers of his familiar world, and tried to picture Louisa as she might be at that moment. Sewing, perhaps, or she might be reading. She was a great reader.

"I'd do anything for her!" he thought. "Well, almost anything," he told himself, more sensibly.

Going ashore at the ferry dock, Van Wempel asked the way to the farmers' market. Nearly four miles to walk—a bit more than he remembered, but he was in the prime of life and he could do it easily.

Trudging through the snow, Van Wempel whistled happily as he recalled the events of the past year—meeting Louisa at a party, falling rapidly and deliriously in love with her, getting the sweetest hints that she might love him too, meeting her parents, proposing, being accepted, buying a suit for the wedding. . . .

Van Wempel was too busy with these memories to notice that he had taken a wrong turn in the gathering dusk. Suddenly he realized that he was walking past a lonely row of boarded-up houses, almost a deserted village. But he could see lights ahead, and hear people talking, so he pushed on until he found them.

Beyond the houses, several wagons had stopped where two lanes crossed, and men he took to be farmers were transacting business of some kind by lantern light. Approaching them, Van Wempel saw that one was holding a pair of noisy white geese under his arms.

"Excuse me," Van Wempel said, "but I would like very much to buy a goose for dinner."

"These two are sold already," the farmer replied.

"Do you have others, perhaps?" Van Wempel continued.

"I've got a Canada goose I could sell you," said the farmer, "but he may not be what you want."

"What's a Canada goose?" Van Wempel asked.

"Big bird, brown feathers, lots of solid meat on him," the farmer said. "He must have been in one of them Vs flying south for the Winter, but he hurt his wing some way, and landed in my pond two months ago."

"I'll take him," said Van Wempel.

They agreed on the price, which was quite a bargain, and the farmer drove away. Van Wempel tried to carry the goose under his arm, but the big bird was too heavy for him. The goose seemed willing enough to accompany him on foot, however, so Van Wempel walked back down the dark country lane with the goose waddling beside him. As he passed the closed-up houses again, he caught a whiff of woodsmoke on the wind, and wondered who might be living in this desolate place.

Suddenly a door opened and a nasty-looking man lurched out onto the road, grabbing Van Wempel by the shoulder.

"Here he is!" the fellow shouted to others inside. "Come to bring us our New Year's goose now, hasn't he?"

Van Wempel twisted out of the man's heavy grip. Courteously but firmly, he explained that the goose was for nobody but his wife, and he must hurry home. At first the man tried to bargain with him, blocking his path.

"Give you half a gallon of the best hard cider you ever did taste," the man offered. "Give you two half a gallons—two halves of a gallon," he added, as Van Wempel continued to refuse.

"Well, I guess we'll have to take your goose then, won't we?" said the man, turning nasty again.

He pushed Van Wempel into the house, where three other rough-looking men were sitting on the floor near a glowing wood stove, playing cards. They stood up quickly to join in this new game, and Van Wempel was frightened—nobody near to help him, nothing to defend himself with. As the ruffians advanced, he backed slowly into the farthest corner of the empty room. Beside him, the goose started hissing at their foes. When one got too close, the goose struck swiftly with his beak and the fellow leaped away. Again, the angry goose drove him back, striking at arm or leg, as the other rascals watched. Van Wempel felt a surge of hope, but there were four of them—this couldn't go on much longer.

He looked around desperately and saw something standing in the corner, an old wooden rake with a long handle. Van Wempel picked the thing up and held it behind him like a hockey stick, ready to swing at them.

"Let me go peacefully, with my goose," said Van Wempel loudly, "or I will have to hurt you."

The four men laughed at that, drew knives from their belts, and edged closer to him. Instead of retreating, however, Van Wempel swung his weapon furiously,

whacking anyone he could reach. Van Wempel's goose stood beside him, hissing and striking with his beak. *Ouch! Ouch! Ouch!* Three of the ruffians fled. The last one remained, slashing to the left, to the right, so close that Van Wempel could see the red light of rage in his eyes. Van Wempel didn't care—with his goose at his side he was advancing now, yelling at the fellow and whacking him, through the open doorway and out into the lane.

"I told you (*whack!*) this goose belongs (*whack!*) to my dear wife (*whack!*) and I'm going (*whack!*) to take it (*whack!*) to her now" (*whack, whack!*).

Van Wempel and his goose stood together in the lane, watching the last of the

defeated ruffians slink away. The night was dark, but the winter moon had climbed higher in the sky, and Van Wempel had no difficulty finding his way back to the ferry dock, the big goose walking beside him.

When he finally got home, Van Wempel embraced his wife even more warmly than usual. He hesitated to tell her that he didn't have the heart to kill the brave goose.

"What's that good smell?" he asked.

"A ham I'm baking for tomorrow," Louisa replied.

"Ham? I thought you wanted goose."

"No, my dear," she explained. "After you left I realized I was being selfish. If ham and turkey are what you want for dinner, then ham and turkey you'll have."

Van Wempel's goose took up residence in the small back yard and guarded the place whenever they were out. He seemed contented enough, but as Spring approached he scanned the sky more and more often. One fine day, his injury fully mended, the goose honked loudly at Van Wempel. Then he spread his powerful wings, and flew up to join the Vs of others like him flying north.

Cloud-Carrier and the Star Folk

A modest young man once lived with his parents near Lake Huron, in what is now called Michigan. According to the customs of his people, the Algonquin Indians, he was sent out alone at a certain age to find proofs of his courage and skills, and to learn what name he would bear as an adult. Exactly how to do this was never explained, so he fell asleep confused after a long day of wandering through the deep forest.

"Cloud-Carrier, I have come to lead you! Follow me!"

Not sure whether he was awake or still dreaming, the young man stumbled to his feet. There before him stood a young woman of such dazzling beauty that his eyes hurt, and he had to look away. The young woman must have understood this, for somehow she reduced her radiance to a soft glow. When he could see her clearly, his heart leaped. She smiled and took his hand.

"Cloud-Carrier, follow me," she repeated.

The young woman ascended from the ground swiftly, effortlessly, and Cloud-Carrier discovered that he could do likewise. Together they flew higher than tree-tops, higher than distant hills, until the great lakes were no larger than teardrops, and the stars seemed to be rushing towards them.

"We must not enter the heavens," Cloud-Carrier cried out in alarm. "The gods will be terribly angry!"

But they did enter the heavens, passing through an opening in the vast dome that covered the earth, and there was no immediate punishment. Instead, a mysterious aura of peace and harmony surrounded them. Cloud-Carrier's beautiful guide, Nemissa, showed him the way to walk lightly on the upper surface of the heavenly dome, which was carved out of purest crystal and surprisingly strong. Gradually he realized that she must be one of the gods herself.

"Who makes the light of the stars?" he asked her.

"The Star Folk," she replied.

She increased her own radiance slightly. Cloud-Carrier could see other figures in the distance, presumably Star Folk, and some buildings which resembled the lodges of his own people.

"NEMISSA!"

Suddenly a voice boomed like thunder, so loud that Cloud-Carrier feared the very dome of the heavens might shatter. It held firm, however, and he saw approaching them a gigantic warrior of the Star Folk, carrying an enormous bow and a handful of arrows resembling bolts of lightning. Comets swirled around this giant's head, buzzing and sparkling, but he slapped them away as though they were irritating flies.

"NEMISSA! HOW DARE YOU BRING AN EARTH PERSON INTO OUR MIDST? HAVE YOU FORGOTTEN THE RULES?"

The young goddess shrank away from this terrifying warrior, and as she did so her radiance faded to almost nothing, while his increased to an angry ball of fire. Cloud-Carrier, having no weapons with him, prayed for help. Then he pictured how stars could be dimmed by the passage of rain-filled clouds. He stood up boldly, facing the angry Star Warrior, and passed his hand across the space between them, as though he were drawing a curtain. Instantly the light and heat flowing from the Star Warrior were diminished, and Nemissa looked at Cloud-Carrier with admiration.

"You are just as brave as I imagined you," she said.

"You imagined me?" Cloud-Carrier replied.

He was amazed, for he was merely one of many Earth People with no special skills or strengths that he knew of. But Nemissa believed otherwise, and Cloud-Carrier soon changed his mind. He remained in the heavens with her for a whole year, using his gift to soften the light or reduce the heat of the heavenly stars when they might be too much for people on earth. Thus he became one of the first humans ever to interfere directly in the affairs of the gods.

At the end of their year together it was time for him to go home. Cloud-Carrier agreed to return to the heavens whenever Nemissa signaled that he was really needed. He slid down a beam of starlight, landing near his village. There he lived simply among the people of his tribe, watching each night for the shooting stars which would tell him the goddess Nemissa was coming to get him again.

Christopher Columbus in the Sea of Gloom

Christopher Columbus wasn't the first European explorer to sail across the Atlantic Ocean in search of other worlds, but he thought he was. His men thought so, too. What set him apart from them went much deeper. He was propelled by faith and ambition of the profoundest kind, while most of his sailors were held back by fears of horrible things that might await them in the "Sea of Gloom," the western reaches of the Atlantic. When they weren't busy working the ships, they told each other stories about ravenous sea monsters, overwhelming storms, whirlpools that could suck them under, and worst of all, an abrupt "edge" where the flat surface of the earth itself would drop away into airy nothing, and they would fall forever—or end up in the fires of Hell. The farther from Spain their three little ships went, the more frightened these poor sailors became.

Finally, on October 11, 1492, the captains of the *Niña* and the *Pinta* sent signals to Columbus on the *Santa Maria*, asking him to stop for a conference. The sea was calm that afternoon, and the two captains easily rowed themselves across to his flagship in small skiffs. Squeezing into the tiny cabin where Columbus kept his records and charts, they reported that the crews of their two ships were close to mutiny. Columbus admitted that his crew was becoming uneasy also. But then he offered to show his

captains the official logbook in which he had been keeping track of the distance traveled each day, from noon to noon.

"We are not too far from home," he assured them. "And soon we will be sailing among the islands of Asia. So tell your men there is absolutely nothing to worry about."

"Our thanks, and blessings be upon you, Don Cristoforo," they responded.

The two captains returned to their ships, and the fleet of three resumed its journey. Music and laughter drifted across the water—startling sounds after the weeks of uncertainty and fear. Columbus realized his deception was working, but moments later the depressing chill of the gloomy sea must have struck him. Shivering, he sought the privacy of his cabin, fell to his knees, and prayed.

"Dear God," he began, "forgive me for telling falsehoods to my honest followers."

It seems that Columbus actually had two different logbooks on his ship. The first one contained the true record of distances traveled, as he had calculated them each day. The second logbook, which he had used to deceive the captains of the *Niña* and the *Pinta,* contained a false record of shorter distances, adding up to less than half of the total miles shown in the first.

What was the right thing to do? Sail on, for the glory of God and Spain, or turn back before it was too late? He couldn't decide. Having prayed until his knees ached, without much easing the ache in his heart, Columbus crawled into bed after midnight and slept fitfully for three hours, his dreams as frightening and exhausting as the fears of his men.

When he awoke again, his candle had gone out, but he could feel the ship rushing through the water as a strong breeze drove it westward. Pulling on his boots and cape to go on deck, Columbus thought he had never seen a sky so dark and gloomy. Darkness on the water, darkness rising like a cliff above his ship—what an infernal place was this awful Sea of Gloom! He closed his eyes and wept with despair. Oh, God! He must give up this great adventure now, and return shamefully to Spain.

"Land ho!" his lookout shouted from the crow's nest above him.

"Land ho!" came the echoes from the other two ships.

Columbus opened his eyes just as the first light of dawn revealed that his fleet had sailed perilously close to a huge land mass. Its steep cliffs and looming mountains still darkened the sky, but now he could see the white flashes of surf breaking on a beach. When he landed there after sunrise, amidst great rejoicing, Columbus named this place San Salvador, because he and his men had been saved from what they feared. Much later he realized he was nowhere near his original destination—Asia was halfway around the globe from this tropical region—but it was bright and beautiful, and the air was full of promise.

Jean Lafitte, the Hero of New Orleans

Jean Lafitte was the world's busiest pirate, and some would say the most successful. In the early 1800s he captured scores of merchant vessels, squeezing millions of dollars out of them. He did so by selling nearly everything he stole—cargoes, cannons, the ships themselves, sometimes even their passengers and crews—in the lawless ports of the Caribbean Sea. Lafitte's treasure chests, stuffed with gold and silver coins, were buried on islands and beaches from the Bahamas to Texas, and mostly forgotten. If Lafitte kept any maps or records of the locations, they were lost when he died. During his lifetime, however, he seems to have kept his followers loyal by handing out small shares of treasure once in a while, and promising more.

To celebrate his piratical success, Lafitte liked to visit the city of New Orleans, where he felt at home among the French-speaking people. He would walk through crowded streets without an escort, splendidly dressed in stolen finery, and give away money as he pleased. The people welcomed him gladly, because of his astonishing boldness and generosity, though some of the officials took a different view. Lafitte was a criminal, after all, who should be brought to justice for his numerous crimes.

But this was easier said than done. At one point Governor Claiborne of Louisiana posted a reward for his arrest. When Lafitte heard about Claiborne's action he put up his own notice, offering a much larger reward for the arrest of the Governor! Nobody took Lafitte's offer seriously except Claiborne himself, who sent gunboats up the coast to capture the pirate at the fortified village of Barataria. Like other efforts, this one met with no success.

Jean Lafitte might have continued his life of crime indefinitely if fate had not intervened. In 1812, the British rulers decided to try again to defeat their former colonies—now the United States of America—and declared war. One of their principal targets was New Orleans, from which the Mississippi River and much of the interior of the new nation could be controlled. A number of battles were fought, but the American navy and coastal defenses were not overcome. After two years of failure, the frustrated British admirals devised a new scheme—military rank and other inducements would be given to Lafitte, if he and his men agreed to come into the war and fight on their side.

What the British didn't know was that Lafitte hated their country because of how it had treated France, his native land, in the European wars recently ended. Now he saw an opportunity to do the armed forces of Britain great harm. From his stronghold at Barataria, Lafitte sent a detailed letter to his old enemy, Governor Claiborne, telling him about the British plans and saying he would rather fight on the American side. *"I am the stray sheep wishing to return to the fold,"* Lafitte wrote. Claiborne was convinced. He talked with Andrew Jackson, the commanding general of the American forces, then invited Lafitte to join them.

In the spectacular battle that followed, a fleet of British warships fired their long-range cannons at American forts all day and all night. The forts fired back, but most of the gunners were Lafitte's men. French and Spanish and Dutch and who knows what other nationalities, their aim was deadly after years of experience as pirates. *Bam! Ba-blam! Bam! Bam!* the American guns roared. One after another, British frigates exploded or burned and sank, until the remainder of the fleet withdrew in defeat.

A short time later, news from Washington reached the joyful city. Peace had been declared! In fact, the war had officially ended before this battle of New Orleans started—but that didn't stop the boisterous citizens from celebrating or expressing their gratitude to Lafitte. Music filled the air, and people in costumes were everywhere, dancing and singing. Lafitte, their hero, made speeches on the same platforms with Governor Claiborne and General Jackson, who soon grew tired of hearing him talk.

And there was more news—the President of the United States had recently issued a proclamation, giving Lafitte and his men full pardons for all of their crimes up to January 8, 1815. Some of the pirates came ashore for good. Lafitte himself was pleased, and he lived quietly for a while, but he returned to piracy later because he honestly couldn't think of anything else to do.

Casey Jones and the Train Wreck

John Luther Jones, known as "Casey" because he came from Casey, Kentucky, was a high-spirited boy who grew up to be a cheerful giant of a man—six feet four and a half inches in his stocking feet. He began working on the Illinois Central Railroad at an early age, and was soon famous for getting his trains to their final destinations on time. This may not seem like much of an accomplishment today, but in the 1890s it was very hard to do. Locomotives frequently broke down, tracks were torn up or flooded, switches froze, and other things happened so that trains were usually late when they started out. The test of a real train driver, or "engineer," was how much of the lost time he could make up before reaching the end of the run. Casey Jones got to be better at this than any other engineer. His skill, success, and plain old good luck would have made him a legend even if he hadn't died young.

The last chapter of his story began around midnight on April 29, 1900. Casey had just driven a freight train into the railroad yards at Memphis, Tennessee, when he heard that a friend of his was sick and couldn't drive another freight that should have left at 11:35 P.M. Nobody else was available on short notice, so Casey offered to drive that train, and his partner, Sim Webb, came along to shovel the coal. Sim, one of the secrets of Casey's success up to that point, was a powerful black man who had worked with him for years.

That foggy night, Casey and Sim had to get from Memphis to Canton, Mississippi, more than two hundred miles, through country that had been flooded by two weeks of rain. Because of all the delays they left Memphis 90 minutes behind schedule. Normally it would have taken at least five hours to reach the end of the line. They were going to try to do it in three and a half hours, non-stop.

Casey drove the train hard, his right hand on the throttle to regulate speed, his left hand on a cord that released steam from the engine to blow a warning whistle. His special tune was a long mournful sound that rose like a trumpet solo as the train rushed along, then died away. That night, making up for so much lost time, he played it often.

While Casey drove, one eye on the clock, Sim fed coal into the big engine, shoveling faster than he ever had before. He was watching the clock too. Later he recalled how rapidly they had been catching up with the schedule as their long freight train flew past country towns in the quiet hours before dawn.

Sardis, Mississippi, 72 minutes behind schedule.

Grenada, 45 minutes.

Winona, 34 minutes.

Durant, 16 minutes.

And soon they were approaching Vaughan, Mississippi, only six and a half minutes late. Sim and Casey grinned, and relaxed for a moment. At this rate, they would pass the next station on time, and pull into Canton bang on schedule.

As their train sped around a sharp curve at Vaughan, Casey and Sim yelled at each other. Another train was stopped dead on the track ahead of them—no one is quite sure why, to this day. The last car was a caboose, a kind of cabin on wheels for the train's crew. Was anyone in there? Casey slammed on the brakes and blew his whistle, but it was impossible to stop in time.

"Jump, Sim, save yourself!" he cried.

Sim dove into the darkness, rolled down an embankment, hit his head and passed out, just as the noise of the crash rolled over him. Cars of both trains were derailed, the empty caboose was splintered, Casey's engine exploded, and Casey himself was killed instantly—just six minutes short of being on time at his final destination.

Sim Webb and a crew member from the other train lived to tell the story of Casey Jones. Later it became a poem, which was set to music and passed along from one train crew to the next. They loved it because it was about them, as well as him:

"Headaches and heartaches and all kinds of pain
Are not apart from a railroad train;
Tales that are earnest, noble and gran'
Belong to the life of a railroad man."

Other Tales of Heroines and Heroes

Mike Fink was the hero of many a tall tale during the early nineteenth century. Compared to other men who worked the flat cargo boats along the Mississippi River, Mike could do most things better than most other men. When he couldn't do something, he said he could, for Mike was also an untoppable braggart. "I can out-run, out-jump, out-shoot, out-brag, out-drink, an' out-fight, rough-an'-tumble, no holts barred, ary man on both sides the river from Pittsburgh to New Orleans an' back ag'in to St. Louiee," he would say, just to get the conversation started. Eventually he became a trapper and trader, followed the American frontier westward, and bragged his last brag in Montana at the age of fifty-nine.

Another fellow who could do almost anything was Alfred Stormalong, a farmer turned sailor out of Boston, Massachusetts. Once when his whaling ship wouldn't move, Stormalong jumped overboard and found a giant octopus holding onto the anchor. Within two or three minutes the ship was freed. Stormy explained that he had simply tied the creature's arms in slip-knots from which it could easily escape. He later served on the last great sailing vessel, the *Courser*, which was so big that men rode horses to move quickly around the deck. Stormy saved many lives when this ship was eventually wrecked, then went ashore to try his hand at farming again.

Belle Boyd turned seventeen years old as the Civil War began. Near her home in Martinsburg, West Virginia, Belle overheard Union officers talking. She slipped through the enemy's lines and reported their plans to the Confederate general, who used this information to defeat them. For this and other daring acts, Belle was celebrated as a heroine in the South. Finally captured, she had to be escorted to prison by 450 Union cavalrymen to prevent her admirers from attempting a dramatic rescue. In solitary confinement she communicated with other prisoners by wrapping messages around marbles and rolling them down the corridor from her cell. She was soon released on parole and allowed to go home, having promised to spy no more.

Harriet Tubman, a black slave, escaped to the North in 1849. She voluntarily returned to the South many times, at great risk to herself, enabling hundreds of other escaping slaves to travel the "Underground Railroad" from one secret place of refuge to the next. During the Civil War, acting more openly, she helped to liberate an additional 800 slaves in South Carolina. When they hesitated to go aboard the waiting ships, Tubman improvised a cheerful song as she led them forward to freedom.

A sixth-century Irish monk, St. Brendan the Navigator, had visions of "the Promised Land" to the west. He selected his crew, built a sturdy boat of leather hides stretched on oak ribs, and sailed northward past the Scottish islands, then westward to Iceland, Greenland, and beyond. Along the way he encountered severe weather and saw things unfamiliar to him, such as whales, icebergs, and volcanoes. After several attempts he ultimately reached his destination—somewhere on the coast of North America—only to find that Irish-speaking people were settled there already.

Phoebe Anne Oakley Mozee, born in Ohio in 1860, became known as "Little Sure Shot" because of her consistent accuracy with pistols and rifles while still a child. Later she joined Buffalo Bill's Wild West Show as "Annie Oakley" and went on tour. Besides demonstrating her astonishing skills in solo performances, she also played the heroine's part in make-believe dramas such as stagecoach holdups, bank robberies, and mock battles between cowboys and Indians. Often it was Annie who saved the day, to the audience's delight, by sharp-shooting her way out of trouble. *Annie Get Your Gun*, a Broadway musical, made her famous again in the 1940s.

Deganawidah was a modest hero whose deeds were overshadowed by those of another Iroquois Indian named Hiawatha, who assisted him. During the sixteenth century, when the five great Iroquois tribes were continuously fighting among themselves, Deganawidah used his diplomatic ability to settle their differences. With his guidance, the warlike Cayugas, Mohawks, Oneidas, Onondagas, and Senecas formed the League of Five Nations to live peacefully together in what is now New York State.

Louis Diamond joined the U.S. Marines in 1917 and served with distinction for almost thirty years, achieving the rank of sergeant during World War II. "Leatherneck Lou" was combative and competitive, whether in battle, sports, or card games, yet he always looked after his men. Repeatedly cited for bravery, Lou was severely wounded at Tulagi and evacuated to a hospital in New Zealand. From there he could have gone home for a hero's welcome. Instead he hitchhiked thousands of miles across the Pacific on military planes and ships to rejoin his buddies for yet another fight.

Kate Shelley, aged fifteen, lived near Boone, Iowa, beside the railroad tracks on which her father had worked before he died. One rainy night in 1881 the Des Moines River was overflowing, and Kate feared that the big railroad bridge would be washed away. She crawled 500 feet across this shaky wooden structure on her hands and knees, then ran to the next train station to give warning. The midnight express was flagged down, avoiding a terrible wreck, and Kate received several rewards, including a lifetime pass on the Chicago & Northwestern and the right to have trains stop just for her as they passed her home.

For general information about heroic American men and women, see Dixon Wechter's *The Hero in America* or Marshall Fishwick's *The American Hero: Myth and Reality*. More specific references include Kent Steckmesser's *The Western Hero in History and Legend*, Elizabeth Ellet's *Pioneer Women of the West*, and B. A. Botkin's *Civil War Treasury of Tales, Legends and Folklore*.

OTHER COLORFUL CHARACTERS

Rosie the Riveter

Try as she would, Rose O'Farrell could never catch up with her older brother, Tom. He wasn't that much older—only a year, ten months, and nineteen days—but he always seemed to be several jumps ahead of her. He was the best speller, the fastest runner, the most decorated Boy Scout in the history of Newton, Massachusetts. He played varsity football and baseball in high school, while Rosie had to be content with field hockey and cheerleading. At graduation, Tommy O'Farrell was voted "boy most likely to succeed" by the class of 1938. Two years later, Rosie's votes were split between "friendliest girl" and "class wit."

With the war coming, Tommy applied to OCS, Officer Candidate School, but discovered that his old football injuries ruled him out. Instead he went right to work at an aircraft factory, as a riveter's apprentice. Two years later, Rosie had to share a job in a flower shop with her oldest friend, Fern Feldman. Fern worked mornings, Rosie afternoons.

Mr. Feldman, who owned the flower shop, was delighted to have both of the girls working there. "The Fern and the Rose," he used to say. "A lovely combination." He took a great interest in the war that was spreading through Europe and Asia, but he was too old for military service himself, so he told the girls and anyone else who would listen that his personal assignment was "to keep the home front beautiful." At this he was very successful.

Rosie learned to choose, trim, and arrange flowers nicely, and often she delivered them on her way home, since the man who used to do that was now in the Navy.

Rosie had never paid much attention to flowers before, and she was glad to learn what enjoyment they brought to people who received them—mostly women left behind in the war, or elderly couples.

The notes that went with the flowers were interesting too. In 1940 they would say things like "Miss you lots already—I'll get home before you know it." Gradually they changed to "Happy Birthday, Love," or "Happy Anniversary, Darling—next year we'll be together again."

After eighteen months of this, Rosie could tell that the war was going to drag on for a long time. Her brother would probably be safe now, but she hated the idea that other boys she knew were enlisting or being drafted. Yet it was strangely exciting to meet boys she didn't know—soldiers and sailors and marines and airmen on their way overseas in fresh, clean uniforms. Rose and Fern would get dressed up after work and go to the USO in Boston, where they could take their pick of hundreds of nice-looking young men to dance with. Fern preferred the foxtrot, occasionally a tango or a rhumba. Rosie loved to jitterbug, swinging higher and higher, until she felt like she was flying.

Then Tommy announced to his family that he had found a way to get into the war after all, driving ambulances for the British army in North Africa. Strictly as an unpaid volunteer. Rosie was speechless with surprise, while Mr. and Mrs. O'Farrell looked both pleased and frightened.

"The recruiter asked me two questions," Tommy recalled with a smile. "Did I have a driver's license and was I breathing? I told him I'll drive anything on wheels."

"Until that shoulder of yours acts up again," his father said gloomily.

But Tommy could not be discouraged or held back. Two days later, packed and ready to shove off, he gave his sister a hug and a kiss.

"You going to stick with the flower shop?" he asked.

"I guess," Rosie replied tearfully.

"Then who's going to fill my shoes?"

"At the aircraft factory?"

"Where else, Sis?" said Tom impatiently. "I'm not talking about the boys' locker room at Newton High."

He was out the door before Rosie could ask him anything else about his old job, but she lay awake for hours that night, wondering, thinking, planning. The next day, before going to work at the flower shop, she took a bus to the aircraft factory and found the personnel office. She realized immediately that high heels, a short skirt, and a rather tight sweater were big mistakes.

The man behind the desk whistled when he saw her, and grinned wolfishly.

"If legs could do it, honey, I'd give you every job in the plant, but I have to say this, you just don't look like a riveter to me."

"What does a riveter look like?" Rosie said sourly.

"Come on, I'll show you."

He led her down the corridor to a window overlooking the production floor of the factory. Dozens of workers were swarming in and out and around large sections of aluminum wings and fuselages. The screaming of high-speed drills and the zipping, thudding sounds of rivet guns were very loud, even through thick glass.

"Where are the women?" Rosie shouted.

"That's my point," the man replied. "You can't tell which is which without a scorecard."

Rosie looked more closely at the busy workers down below. Some wore shapeless coveralls, others were disguised by welding masks. The rest were more or less uniformly dressed in trousers and shirts. Among them she began to pick out females by their postures or their ways of walking. Some wore makeup, earrings, and scarves or bandanas on their hair.

"I get the idea, thanks," Rosie said to the personnel man.

"I'll be back," she added to herself. She was glad that she hadn't given her name or filled out any papers yet.

After delivering some flowers that evening, Rosie stood before the bathroom mirror at home and wiped every trace of makeup from her face. Her lips were still full and  pink, and her eyes still big and blue, but the movie-star look was gone. She took her earrings off and twisted an ugly plaid scarf around her curly red hair.

"That's better," Rosie thought.

She went into Tommy's room, found a couple of his blue workshirts, and put one on, tucking it loosely into her baggiest pair of slacks. A pair of white socks, flat-heeled shoes, a shoulder bag to carry lunch, and Rosie was ready.

"Now I look like a riveter, I guess. The next question is, can I learn to be one?"

Rosie went to work at the factory two days later, after telling Fern and Mr. Feldman the news. She didn't get Tommy's old job, exactly, because for once in her life she could do things that Tommy couldn't have done—crawling inside airplane wings, for instance, to line up holes and drive hot rivets in places only a small-boned person could reach. Within a month, she was no longer just an apprentice. Two months after that, she was ready to head a team of three, but her supervisor called her aside.

"When are you getting married?" he asked.

"I didn't know I was," said Rosie, puzzled.

"Most girls your age have only one thing on their minds, kiddo—falling in love, getting married, and raising a family."

"That's more than one thing," Rosie thought, but she calmly explained that she was going to stick with her job for the duration of the war, at least.

"Don't count on it, kiddo," the supervisor said. "Some GI is going to come home and want his job back, sooner or later. Maybe even that hotshot brother of yours."

"Tommy had his legs blown off by a land mine in Italy," Rosie informed him. "So if you've got no more words of wisdom, I'll go back to work."

"I'm sorry . . ."

Rosie worked grimly for the next year. Her team was usually at or near the top of the list for getting the job done quickly and well. The factory produced its one hundredth plane in May 1944, and Rosie was honored by visiting big shots. "Rosie the Riveter" some newspapers labeled her. People from Washington asked if they could use her picture on a recruiting poster. Rosie agreed. But when the artist came to make sketches, he seemed quite disappointed.

"Rosie the Riveter," he mused. "We were imagining a sultry brunette, more of a 'calendar girl,' with big brown eyes and Cupid lips—but a patriotic expression, of course. Would you mind if we tried you in a wig?"

"Yes, I would mind," Rosie said abruptly. "But I used to know somebody who might have just what you're looking for."

She scribbled a name

and telephone number on a slip of paper, and gave it to the artist.

"Here," she said. "And now if you'll excuse me, there's a war on."

Hurrying back to work, she wondered whether she should call Fern Feldman to explain what she had done, or let it go. Better call. Fern's father answered and told Rosie that his daughter had gone overseas three months ago with the Air Transport Command.

"Feldman the Flier," he said proudly. "I'll let her know you phoned."

Billy Earthquake, the Bronco-Buster

Will Urquhart was the roughest, scruffiest, most ornery cowboy who ever sat a horse in the Republic of Texas, back before the Mexican War. He was also the loudest—he'd get drunk, stand on the bar, and brag about himself until the saloon emptied out or somebody was foolish enough to take him on.

"This is *me*, and no mistake!" he'd holler. "William Sinclair Urquhart, Senior, commonly known as 'Billy Earthquake,' come all the way here from San Anton' to see about *you*. I'm no yearling, for sure, but cuss me if I can't still whip any man on this side of the Rio Grande, or the other side neither, for that matter!"

He'd pause to take a sip of his rye whiskey, and usually the crowd was quiet.

"Wahoo! Won't *nobody* stand up and fight me? Come on, some of you, and fight decently. I'm spiling for a fight! I ain't had one for more than a week, and my joints are starting to go rusty on me. So step right up, boys, and help me out."

Billy would smile, revealing his broken teeth, and unbuckle his heavy gun belts to show that he meant to fight with his fists.

"I'm gettin' to be an old man, it's a fact, and I smell like a wet dog, but I can't be run over! I'm the one who threw a rope around a whole herd of steers, and towed them across the flooded river, while the rest of the cowboys just sat and watched. I can bend a new horseshoe into shape with nothin' but the heat of my temper! And speaking of horses—there ain't a bronc been born I couldn't ride. If anyone denies it, let 'im speak right now. Cock-a-doodle-doo!"

At this point some newcomer might venture to say a word, and Billy would make short work of him—pull his hat down over his ears, or slap him backhanded a couple of times, or twist the man's knife out of his hand and offer to carve his turkey for dinner. Then back to bragging.

"Talk about grinning the bark off a cottonwood tree! That ain't nothing worthy of mention. One squint of my eye at the Devil's heel would blister it! Oh, I'm your toughest sort—live forever, and then turn into a white oak post. I'm the gen-u-wine article, the real thing come to Texas in a cloud of glory! I can out-run, out-jump, out-swim, chaw more tobacco and spit less, and drink more whiskey and keep soberer than any man in these parts."

Then Billy would climb down off the bar, lean toward the bartender, and whisper: "If that don't make 'em fight, nothin' can."

Finally came the day when a clean-cut young man stood up to Billy Earthquake as he was about to depart. Billy started his routine all over again, until the young man interrupted.

"I know who you are, well enough," he said.

"And just who might you be?" Billy inquired, squinting at him with one eye shut.

"I'm Will Urquhart, Junior," the young man replied. "I'm your long-lost son."

"Well I'll be a ring-tailed, cross-eyed, double-gaited hog at the back end of a wagon train to nowhere!" Billy hollered. "Are you absotively, posilutely sure?"

"Yes, and I can prove it," young Will replied. He passed a handful of papers to Billy, and the two of them went over to the corner table for a long talk.

After that, Billy took Will out to the open range and put him through some tests—shooting at targets, roping wild horses, and riding.

"You're mighty good," the father told his son, "but you ain't no Billy Earthquake yet. Besides—you don't know how to fight, and you sure can't brag worth a turnip."

Will explained that he didn't want to brag or fight, or do anything much except ride horses.

"All right," said his father, "we'll just set our sights on that."

For several months, Billy taught young Will everything he knew, except the wisdom that Will already had in his head, and the goodness in his heart. Will started entering rodeos, small ones at first, then bigger competitions against the best riders of the Southwest. Whenever he won a prize, Billy would head for the nearest saloon, climb onto the bar, and shout:

"Cock-a-doodle-doo! I'm William Sinclair Urquhart, Senior, better known as the father of Billy Earthquake, Junior, the greatest bronco-buster who ever rode a four-legged bundle of lightning. . . ."

Cinderella of Santa Fe

Once upon a time there was a pretty girl named Gertrudes de Barcelo, who lived with her father and stepmother in the humblest of villages near Santa Fe, New Mexico. Gertrudes planned to become a princess, just as soon as she had saved enough money to leave home. This was no dream—day or night, Gertrudes thought about taking the Trailways bus to Palm Beach, Florida, and marrying a prince! She had found magazine articles on Miami, Tucson, Lake Tahoe, and other fancy resorts, but Palm Beach was the home of the young man who appealed to her the most—Leland J. Costello, the Fourth. She cut out his pictures and kept them in a scrapbook.

Falling asleep at night, Gertrudes imagined her first date with the prince she had chosen for herself. He was tall, gentle, handsome—a curly lock of black hair fell across his brown eyes, and he kept pushing it back. He'd wear a splendid blue blazer, or possibly a fancy uniform, and ask her politely if she could waltz. Of course she could! Gertrudes loved to dance, any step or any tempo. Together they would whirl across the shining floor of the palace ballroom, always in sync, just the two of them, while other couples looked on. But what would she be wearing?

"Wake up, Gertie," her stepmother shouted, "It's one A.M., time to go to work."

"But what would I be wearing?" Gertrudes repeated, still half asleep.

"The same things you always wear, my darling. Blue jeans, a blouse, and sandals."

Gertrudes washed herself, dressed swiftly, and hurried through the dark streets to the old-fashioned dance hall where she worked, cleaning the bathrooms, sweeping up trash, waxing the floor for tomorrow's customers. There were still a few people dancing near the bandstand—girls she knew and officers from the military base. As Gertrudes watched them, the manager of the dance hall approached her.

"I'm sorry, sir," she stammered. "I know I should be working. I'll stay later to make up for it."

"Relax a moment," the manager replied. "You know, Gertie, I've been thinking about you."

Gertrudes had heard this kind of talk from men before, and she waited silently for the rest of it. But the manager surprised her.

"You're a wonderful dancer," he smiled. "I've seen you going around the floor with a mop in your arms, late at night, when nobody else was looking."

"I'm sorry," Gertrudes said. "It won't happen again."

"Oh, but it should happen," the manager replied. "We need another girl around here. To dance with customers. I mean, only to dance with them. Nothing personal, if you understand me."

Gertrudes agreed to try it. The manager's wife would find her a new dress. Her pay would be twice as much as she was making now—she could buy lots of nice clothes and a bus ticket to Palm Beach that much sooner. And dancing! Her thoughts were full of dancing as she did the chores, hour after hour, and trudged home at noon. She ate breakfast to please her adoring stepmother, then fell asleep and dreamed again of being the princess rescued by an elegant prince.

The next evening, Gertrudes changed into a red satin dress. It barely covered her shoulders, and she was embarrassed, but the manager's wife gave her a lacy shawl to wear. Gertrudes entered the hall more excited than she had been in years.

Night after night, Gertrudes danced with men of every variety, including military officers. A few were good-looking, a few could waltz, yet for her it was just another dance in the arms of a stranger—nothing magical about it. Gertrudes longed to hear the gentle voice of her prince, to float around the floor without once having her feet stepped on! She was making plenty of money. As she got closer to leaving Santa Fe, however, the palace in Palm Beach seemed farther and farther away.

Early one morning, as Gertrudes was about to go home, she saw a solitary figure on the floor, dancing with a mop as she used to do. She recognized Fernando, the shy young man who had been hired to take her place cleaning. Tall, black-haired, and barefoot, he moved so gracefully that Gertrudes waited for several minutes before she spoke.

"May I have this dance?"

Fernando looked at her with astonishment, suddenly awakened from his dreams to take flight in the arms of a real princess.

Rip Van Winkle

Rupert Van Winkle and his brother Eze-
kiel were the laziest fellows in Catskill, New York, an old Dutch settlement on the
Hudson River. They had lost their little restaurant business when times were bad, in
the 1890s, and they had nothing to do. Usually they slept through the night and most
of the day, emerging from their untidy cottage at sundown to beg food and drink.

Neighbors would laugh as the two fat brothers waddled down the village street.
"Here come Rip and Zip," they'd say. "Who's going to feed them tonight?"

The brothers lived this way until one foggy evening when the village was closed
up tight, as though everyone had left to escape a plague.

"What shall we do?" Rip asked Zip.

"I haven't a clue," Zip replied.

They huddled on the dark waterfront, feeling hungry and hopeless. After a while
they saw something they hadn't noticed before—alongside the village dock, shroud-
ed in fog, an old ship had come to rest. It looked like a Dutch trading vessel from the
early days, short and stubby, with a lighted cabin rising high above its cluttered deck.
Though the ship was tied up securely, its square-rigged sails were still set for a voyage.

"Shall we try it?" Rip asked.

"Either that or diet," Zip replied.

They climbed a rope ladder from the dock, then found their way slowly up narrow stairways to the top of the stern castle, where glowing lamps beckoned them.

"They must have food," Rip assured Zip.

"They can't be rude," Zip replied.

Entering the cozy cabin, they beheld a table crowded with tempting dishes. Behind it sat a bald-headed man in a faded silk coat. He greeted them courteously, though his accent was hard to understand.

"Velcom gentlemanz velcom zhip, zuch vonderful ztuffz you vill eat," he said.

"An elegant feast," said Rip.

"Ten dinners at least," Zip replied.

Sitting down opposite their bald-headed host, they hungrily attacked the platters of meat, fish, and vegetables, taking frequent sips of a clear beverage that tasted sweeter than honey. Now the old ship was turning into the current of the river, heading south toward Manhattan, but Rip and Zip didn't care.

"A trip in a ship," said one brother, his mouth full of food.

"For Rip and Zip," the other replied.

Later, as full as two fat fellows could possibly get, they were led to featherbeds, where they fell instantly asleep. The next day, awakening earlier than usual, they found themselves anchored in the midst of other sailing vessels, much grander than theirs, with banners saying, "New Amsterdam Festival—Year 2000." Flags of many colors flew from the masts. In the distance were dozens of gleaming buildings that

seemed as tall as the Catskill Mountains. Horseless vehicles roared through the streets, and the noise was incredible.

"Hurry gentlemanz!" cried their host.

They climbed aboard an open cart, pulled by snarling dogs, which plunged into the terrifying traffic and moved along so rapidly that the wheels hardly seemed to touch the pavement. Skidding to a stop at last, they saw what looked like a bowling green. People in old Dutch costumes were practicing. Instead of the usual pins, seven men as fat as themselves cowered in the middle, being struck and knocked down by large wooden balls crashing into them from all directions. Laughter and applause drowned out their cries of pain.

"Two more here, makes nine," their excited host announced, as Rip and Zip were dragged toward the other fat men. "Now game beginz!"

"This must be a dream," said Rip.

"So it would seem," Zip replied.

They struggled wildly to wake up. As they scrambled out of sleep, however, the brothers became separated in time, and neither could return to the year 1900, when their mysterious journey had begun. Rip got safely home, only twenty years after their departure, but Zip missed the starting point by a much wider margin. He went back more than three centuries, landing on a canal bank in Holland to the bewilderment of his stout Van Winkle ancestors.

Fountain of Youth

Juan Ponce de León was a vain young man who sailed with Columbus to the New World in 1492. During that glorious voyage, his black hair grew long and curly, his skin became bronzed, and his boyish voice deepened into a becoming baritone. When he returned to Spain two years later, Juan's good looks caught the attention of many a fair lady, and his stories of high adventure held their interest for many a day.

More voyages, more stories, and always more ladies—it seemed to Juan that fortune would smile upon him forever. But one sunny morning he woke up in the guest room of a Spanish mansion, leaped out of bed, glanced in the mirror, looked again and saw some wrinkles on his previously youthful face. He was getting older! Quickly counting the years, he realized that he was almost middle-aged! *Impossible!* No, not impossible, but totally unacceptable to him.

For weeks Juan tried to hide the truth from others—wearing a big hat that shaded his face, not standing so close to people—but he couldn't hide the truth from himself. *Old!* Sooner or later, a younger man would take his place as the favorite of the ladies, and he would be pushed aside, ignored, forgotten!

Juan did not ask anyone for advice—he feared that men would sneer at his vanity, and women would gossip. So he seized the next opportunity to leave Spain. He sailed back to the New World, where ambition and courage were more important than age or appearance. Juan served his captain well, and was soon given his own ship to command. As he proudly strolled the decks, one of the sailors was telling others about a tropical paradise, island or mainland it wasn't clear, where precious jewels covered the beaches, gold glittered in the streams, and every sort of food and drink could be found without effort.

Juan smiled. He wasn't really listening—until suddenly he heard a word that meant much to him.

"A fountain of what?" he demanded.

"A fountain of youth," the sailor repeated. "Forgive me for talking this foolishness, Excellency."

"You may continue," said Juan. "Such ridiculous ideas are amusing to me."

So the sailor went on with his tantalizing description of a magical fountain. To drink there was to remain forever young. In some cases, he added, youth could be restored to people who had already begun to grow old.

Juan laughed, but he listened closely to every detail about this fountain of youth and its setting "like a pearl in the shell of an oyster."

During the next year, Juan Ponce de León stopped at dozens of small Caribbean islands. They were beautiful, fruitful, charming—but their waters had no magical effects. Then a much larger mass of land was sighted, probably the west coast of Florida near St. Petersburg and Tampa. The ship entered a bay that divided in two, like the halves of an oyster shell. Juan could see a beautiful grove of coconut palms, just where a pearl would be.

"Faster, faster!" he shouted, as the crew rowed him toward the beach.

Leaping ashore, Juan ordered the sailors to remain with the rowboat while he explored. There were several fountains among the palm trees, but one was different from the others. The water looked pearly white, reflecting every detail of his face and body. Through his reflection, however, Juan could see some sort of inscription at the bottom. *"If you drink here,"* it said, *"you will never escape from the joys of youth."*

"Escape?" he cried. "Not I!" Taking off his clothes, he plunged into the water and drank deeply. First he felt strange sensations, then great pleasure. Stretching out on the grass, he fell asleep.

Hours later Juan awoke and rushed down to the beach. The sailors, still waiting for their captain, regarded him curiously.

"What do you want, lad?" one of them asked him.

"I am Ponce de León, you fool!" Juan cried.

But as the sailors laughed, he looked down at himself and realized that he had turned into a child of seven or eight.

"I'm your captain!" he insisted. "Take me out to the ship!"

"No, little one," the sailor replied. "You may become a captain someday, but we can't take you with us now. You are much too young."

Vikings in America

A thousand years ago, when the land we call "America" was still a nameless mystery to most Europeans, some adventurous people known as Vikings left their homes in Scandinavia to cross the Atlantic Ocean in search of this new world. Passing through the islands north of Scotland, they sailed farther and farther westward—their small wooden ships battered by storms, their food and water running low, their dreams distorted by horrible images of sea monsters and threatening gods.

Hundreds of these Viking explorers got as far as Iceland or Greenland before losing their lives or turning back. Only a few reached the coast of our continent somewhere in Canada or New England, calling the place of their arrival "Vineland" because of its natural bounty.

Here they divided into three groups. The first group settled on a hill overlooking the sea, with high log walls for protection. The second group returned to Norway and Sweden, to spread the marvelous news and to recruit more settlers. The third group used the two remaining ships to explore the interior of the new land, following a great river which was probably the St. Lawrence, later discovering the Great Lakes. They got as far west as Lake Superior, in what is now Minnesota, where the deep snows of a severe winter brought them to a halt. Then they had to burn both of their ships in a last desperate attempt to avoid freezing to death. The men gave their food to the women and children, and went off to die alone in the white wilderness. A boy, three girls, and two women were all that survived to see the following Spring.

The boy, Olaf Olafson, lived with his mother and sister in a crude shelter made of interwoven pine boughs. He was only four years old, but he had already learned to find edible berries and roots in the forest, and to pluck small fish from the lake with his bare hands. Olaf had no interest, however, in farming or fishing. He pestered his mother and the other woman with questions about their homeland in Norway. As he got older he tried to persuade them to start building a ship.

"That's impossible, my dear," Olaf's mother told him. "We haven't the knowledge or the tools."

"At least we could make a raft, and float across this lake," he insisted.

"Oh, my son," his mother said with sadness in her voice. "You remind me so much of your father, strong and stubborn. But we are many miles from the sea. And the sea is stronger and more stubborn than you can imagine. A raft would have no chance."

Six years passed, during which Olaf Olafson grew taller and stronger, wiser and more stubborn. Sometimes in the woods he found traces of other humans, but he never saw them, and never mentioned them to his own people, because he did not want to make friends or enemies—he wanted to go back to his Norwegian homeland.

Olaf's sister died of some strange illness, and not long after that his mother also became ill.

"Olaf," she whispered, "I am going soon. Take these things now."

Olaf, showing none of his sorrow, looked down at the two small leather pouches his mother held.

"They were your father's," she said. "Now yours. One is the soil, the other is the seed."

The night after his mother's death, Olaf sat on a bluff above the misty, moonlit lake and opened the two pouches. He fingered dark soil with one hand, smooth pale seeds with the other. Then, acting on impulse, he climbed down to the lake and waded out into the chilly water. Near the shore, rocks and driftwood had accumulated on a narrow island about thirty feet long. At one end of this island, rising through the mist, a large twisted tree stump resembled the ferocious figurehead of a Viking ship his mother had described to him.

Reaching the center of the island, Olaf put his handful of soil into a moist place between rocks, and carefully planted his seeds. He prayed for a moment.

"But I'm not a farmer," Olaf told himself, as he returned to the small Viking camp. He was sure that tall Norwegian trees would sprout like masts on the island some day, that oars would grow there too, and that somehow he or his children or his children's children would find their way back to the sea.

Johnny Appleseed

Stories about Johnny Appleseed are as numerous and scattered as the apple trees he planted when Ohio was still a Territory at the edge of the American frontier. For instance, descendants of the Amariah Watson family had heard about a strange-looking man who approached their isolated farm one summer day in 1812. He walked right into the kitchen, without knocking, and scared young Mrs. Watson half to death. Sitting down at the table where she had been rolling out dough for bread, he blessed her, told her to fear no evil, then tried to explain why he was wearing only one shoe.

"You see, ma'am," he said, holding out his other foot bare, "this one has been guilty of offense in treading unmercifully upon one of God's creatures—a rattlesnake, to be exact—and as a corresponding punishment, I am now exposing it to the inclemency of the weather."

His smile, gentle and reassuring, belied the untidy appearance of tangled hair and ragged, mismatched clothes. He carried an old Bible in his hand and a big leather sack over his shoulder, but no weapons.

As he went on speaking, Mrs. Watson realized who he was, although she had never actually seen Johnny Appleseed before. People described him as a harmless man who appeared in Ohio fairly often, from somewhere else. They called him "Appleseed" because he planted the seeds to start apple orchards on parcels of unclaimed land, then traded them or sold them or simply gave them away to folks more needy than himself.

Johnny Appleseed left the Watson place after a few minutes, having refused any sort of food or drink, but Mrs. Watson saw him fold a handful of seeds into the soft earth of her barnyard before he vanished down the lane. Afterwards she could never bake an apple pie without recalling him.

Many other Ohio families were glad of Johnny Appleseed's visits, because he usually left things better than he found them. And people added to his legend, as they told one another bits and pieces of what he had been saying and doing.

Buying a sick cow or hog, and nursing it back to health.

Fascinating children and comforting the elderly.

Shouting Biblical verses into the echoing wilderness.

Enduring cold and pain as though he couldn't feel them.

Making peace with hostile Indians.

And always planting apple seeds, here, there, and everywhere, from the sack that he carried in a canoe or on someone's old horse or on his own back.

But this was just a patchwork of impressions. Among his contemporaries, nobody seemed to know who Johnny Appleseed really was, where he came from, or why he chose the forests and hills of central Ohio to be his promised land.

The real name of this puzzling man was Jonathan Chapman, and it turns out that he had no roots in the Midwest. He was born in Massachusetts in 1774 or 1775, on the eve of the American Revolution. His parents were poor but devoutly religious people who believed in sharing whatever they had with others, for the love of God. They died when Johnny was still a little boy, and left him nothing. Soon he disappeared into the growing stream of orphans who wandered around the country during those turbulent years—frightened, homeless, starving children, sometimes taken in by other families, sometimes left to fend for themselves.

Johnny survived the terrible hardships of his childhood in New England, and lived to be seventy-two years old, but he never outgrew the habits of a hungry, homeless child. He ate things that other people threw away or fed to animals. Refusing to live indoors, he slept in haystacks and caves, in livestock pens, in hollow trees, seldom the same place more than once until he began to trust people. His footwear and clothing were castoffs and rags, but they changed often as he gave what he had to others. His funny-looking "hat" was the metal pot he sometimes used for cooking. Later, because strong sunlight hurt his eyes, he fashioned a wide sombrero from scraps of paper and wood.

Encouraged by voices that only he could hear, Johnny made his way southward through New York and New Jersey while still in his teens. He worked for food on some of the Amish farms around Lancaster, Pennsylvania. He also learned to read there, and when he left, the German farmers gave him four or five old school books as well

as a heavy Bible. He refused to part with that Bible until the day he died. But he soon figured out a way to share his other books, tearing them into sections of ten or twenty pages, and offering them to different people he met as he went along. If the torn-out pages made no sense to them—if they couldn't read at all—it didn't really matter to Johnny Appleseed. What mattered was the sharing.

From the Amish country he walked westward, following the wagon tracks of pioneers heading for the Ohio frontier. Somewhere beyond the village of Orchard Hills,

Pennsylvania, after sunset, he found a lame horse that had been left to die beside the trail. He wrapped its sore leg in some of his own rags and led it across a valley, through sweet-smelling apple trees, towards the distant lights of a farmhouse. The horse fell asleep standing up, leaning against a tree, and Johnny did likewise to keep him company. The next morning the farmer agreed to care for Johnny's horse in exchange for work—picking apples ten hours a day until the trees were bare.

Johnny was allowed to eat apples freely as he worked, and was pleased that his

horse enjoyed them too. The red, delicious fruit seemed like food from Heaven. After the harvest, he learned, apples could be squeezed in a big wooden thing called a "cider press," to produce the most refreshing drink. Even more interesting was the fact that heaps of apple seeds accumulated in the bottom of the press, and the farmer threw most of them away.

Johnny continued working there, making cider, until his horse was ready to move on. Before he left, Johnny asked if he could take a sackful of apple seeds with him.

"Why?" the farmer asked.

Johnny didn't answer, except to smile, because he didn't know what to say at that moment. But as he rode away the next day, holding the rope he used for reins in one hand and his Bible in the other, he could hear voices telling him where to go next, and what to do. It was just a matter of getting there.

Two days later he came to the Allegheny River, which was so high from autumn rains that his horse couldn't cross it. Nearby several families of Indians had camped. Johnny courteously offered them some apple seeds, which they courteously declined, but through gestures they expressed an

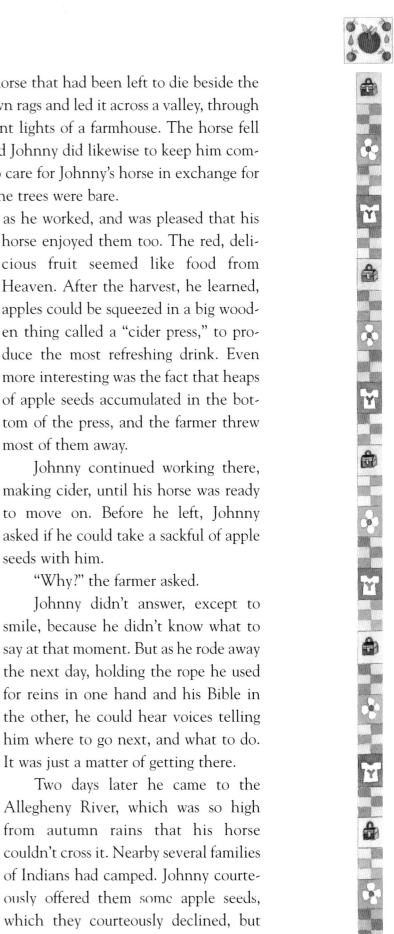

interest in his horse. Usually generous, he hesitated, because he had become fond of the animal. Yet the Indians might need it more than he did.

Trade canoe for horse, they suggested. Still he felt hesitant. Trade two canoes. Yes, he nodded, I'll do that.

So Johnny Appleseed gave the horse a farewell pat and glided down the river with two canoes, towing one and paddling the other as the Indians had shown him. The river became rough, however, and the canoes capsized several times. Then it oc-curred to Johnny to lash them together, side by side, like a double-hulled boat. That is how he managed to survive the rapids where the Allegheny meets the Monon-gahela to form the Ohio River. And that is how he traveled when he left the Ohio, many miles downstream, to follow a network of creeks northward into the land of his legend. Again and again he visited there, bearing gifts.

Years later, barefoot and limping, Johnny Appleseed came out of the woods at lunchtime near Isaac Madden's tumbledown cabin. Madden, an unsuccessful farmer who had borrowed money from everybody for miles around, was reading the Bible to his unfed family as they huddled near the fire.

"Give us this day our daily bread," he prayed.

Johnny Appleseed, entering uninvited, heard these familiar words with a joyful heart.

"And forgive us our debts, as we forgive our debtors," he rejoined.

Isaac Madden jumped up from his bench, surprised, but the three children were very glad to see this visitor.

"It's Johnny Applesauce!" a little girl shouted gleefully. "Do you have a present for me?"

Johnny Appleseed almost always had presents for children, but this time his pockets were nearly empty. Reaching deep, he found a length of pink ribbon, which he cut in two so that the little girl could share it with her older sister. For the boy, however, he could find nothing special, so he opened his leather sack and offered his last handful of apple seeds.

"Plant a tree," he said.

"The tree of life," the boy replied.

"That's it," Johnny agreed ecstatically. "The tree of life."

Headless Horseman

Katrina Van Tassel sat at her dressing table one evening, admiring herself in the gold-framed mirror before going downstairs to dinner. This was her birthday, in the year 1840, and Katrina was now twenty years old—tall and graceful and beautiful—with long blonde braids and the bluest of blue eyes. Her dress was patterned silk, the best that money could buy, blue to match her eyes.

Behind Katrina on the walls of her elegant bedroom were miniature portraits of prosperous relatives—some who had died long ago in Europe, others who had come from the Netherlands to New Amsterdam, as New York was once known, to settle on several thousand acres in the Hudson River Valley, and to develop this land into bountiful farms.

Although she had never gone to school or college, Katrina had been educated by carefully-chosen governesses and tutors, and she happened to be extremely bright. She could discuss things intelligently in any company, no matter what the topics of conversation might be. Sitting between her brothers Hans and Mies after dinner, Katrina would sometimes put them and their friends to shame, although she realized that it was not "lady-like" for a young woman to do so. But she was sorely tempted when they said something stupid!

One young man, Willem Van Dusen, seemed a little brighter than the others. Willem, or "Vim" as her brothers called him, was the best-looking, too, although that was of absolutely no importance to Katrina. He had read some of her favorite books, she found, and he even had an idea or two of his own, about farming or politics or the future of the country, although he didn't want to talk about such things with her.

"Let's not go into that now," Vim would say to Katrina, with a twinkle in his deep brown eyes. "Let's talk about you."

"What about me?" she would reply, although she soon learned what answers to expect. "Your beauty, of course," or "your charm," or sometimes, "the way you look when you're happy."

Katrina liked her own appearance very much, but she got tired of talking about herself this way. So she would try to change the subject, or else she would find an excuse for turning her attention away from Mr. Vim Van Dusen, attractive though he might be. Yet the other young men of her acquaintance were even worse!

"If I had two wishes," Katrina said to herself, "first I would be rid of this annoying freckle on the tip of my nose—and second, I would find someone truly interesting to talk to."

She never got her wish about the freckle. It stayed with her all the rest of her days, although it faded a little when she was older. But she did get her other wish, in an unexpected way. A new schoolmaster came to their village, a bright young man from Brooklyn. He promptly paid a call on her father, who had put up most of the money to hire him.

Katrina overheard part of their conversation from the hall, and she was amazed. This fellow could talk about anything—mathematics, geography, poetry, even corn and wheat! And her father obviously liked him—she could tell from the roars of laughter as the two of them talked.

Walking out into the large and splendid garden, Katrina imagined that her hero had come to rescue her from boredom. She pictured him as tall, extremely good-looking, perhaps taller and better-looking than Vim—but far too interested in ideas to care about his looks! Katrina was sure that he would need a haircut, and his clothes would be old and wrinkled and dusty. Nothing a woman's touch couldn't fix, of course.

But the young fellow who came out later to introduce himself to her was no romantic hero. Tall, yes. Needing a haircut and a good spring cleaning, yes. But as far from handsome as any man could get—he looked like an overgrown chicken, with a small head perched on top of a clumsy body, and a large Adam's apple that bobbed up and down as he spoke.

"How d'you do, Miss Van Tassel," he blurted out in a strangled voice. "My name is Ichabod Crane. . . ."

Katrina couldn't remember what he said after that, or what she might have said to him. All she could think of was his incredible ugliness, his clumsiness—he stumbled repeatedly as he walked beside her in the garden. But after he had departed, Katrina thought more about him, and criticized herself. What did it matter if Ichabod

Crane was ugly or clumsy? She was surrounded by fine-featured, graceful young men who failed to interest her. At least this schoolteacher could talk!

The next time Ichabod came to visit, Katrina ignored his looks and paid close attention to what he said. He seemed to know something about everything, and when he spoke, the words poured out of him in a rapid, twisting stream. He talked, Katrina listened, and occasionally she asked questions.

"But why do the planets revolve around the sun?" she might say. And Ichabod would tell her the answer. "How does a river like the Hudson make such a deep valley?" And he would explain it to her.

Ichabod Crane came to visit more and more often. He looked at Katrina intently while they talked. His ugly face lit up whenever she smiled at him. Sometimes when he left he would take with him a flower that Katrina had picked in the garden, or a bit of paper on which she had written a few words. Katrina herself was too busy talking and thinking to notice these things. But other people did notice them, including her two brothers and their friend Vim Van Dusen. Hans and Mies thought it was amusing for Katrina to be so deeply interested in nothing but words, words, and more words. Mr. Van Dusen, however, was not amused.

"That scarecrow!" he muttered to himself. "That poor excuse for a man! He has no right to be making goo-goo eyes at my Katrina!"

Vim Van Dusen was jealous. But he was smart enough to conceal his jealousy from everyone—especially from Ichabod Crane. Instead he pretended to like the young teacher, who had almost no friends. He loaned Ichabod an old brown horse, and made sure he could ride it. He took Ichabod fishing. While they fished, he told Ichabod stories about ghosts and witches and other strange creatures that lived in the woods and came out at night—especially Brom Bones, the headless horseman. He described this apparition in gory detail—the neck cut clean across by the stroke of a saber, the head dripping blood.

"But that's scientifically impossible, Vim!" cried Ichabod. "A person can't ride a horse if he has no head."

"I'm telling you, Ichabod, I've seen Brom Bones with my own eyes," Vim replied. "He rides this river road by the light of the full moon, and he carries his head underneath his arm."

"Impossible," Ichabod repeated. "Scientifically impossi-ble." But he shuddered with fear, and Vim Van Dusen smiled to himself.

A few nights later, when the moon was full, Vim arranged to meet Ichabod at the river to fish for eels. Ichabod, arriving late as usual, tethered his horse and dropped his fishing rod. As he stooped to pick it up, he heard another horse thundering

towards him down the road. Around the bend it came galloping, huge and white in the moonlight, its rider wearing an old military costume—headless! Yes, headless, and there floating above him was . . . his head! And it was dripping!

Ichabod Crane didn't stop for a scientific explanation—he jumped on his own horse and fled. At home he threw his books and other belongings into the sack he used instead of a suitcase. Then he wrote a letter to the village officials, making up a reason for his sudden departure. After that Ichabod tried to calm down and sleep, but every time he dozed off, the most horrible dreams would seize his imagination—horses and riders chasing one another, and a big clumsy chicken running around with its head cut off . . .

In the morning Ichabod rode his old brown horse to Albany, where he could catch the next boat sailing down to Manhattan. As they pulled away from the dock, Ichabod felt better. He looked back at the neat houses, beyond them the sunlit fields of the big Dutch farms, and realized he should have left a note for Katrina.

"Oh well," he thought. "Perhaps I shall correspond with her later."

But he forgot to write, and Katrina gradually forgot about poor Ichabod Crane. She spent more and more time in the pleasing company of Vim Van Dusen. He could talk about some of her favorite books, as they walked or rode or danced together, and he had an idea or two of his own. All he needed, Katrina realized, was a woman's touch to draw him out.

Windwagon Thomas

Thomas O'Bannion was a saltwater sailor from Ireland, like his father and grandfather before him. He loved the boundless freedom of the ocean, the sky, the winds—it was hard for Thomas when his ship finally reached land and he had to go ashore while cargo was unloaded, repairs made, and supplies carried aboard for the next voyage. Walking around the streets of London or Hong Kong, New York or Valparaiso, he found little color or interest in what he saw, and he could hardly wait to escape the limited horizons of city life.

But one day in New Orleans he met a young man who talked about building flatboats—those small wooden barges, pulled by mules or pushed by poles, that were just right for shallow waters such as the rivers feeding into the Mississippi. The young man was looking for a partner to help him get rich.

"We'll put *wheels* on flatboats," he said, "so they can be used as wagons as well, and sell them to all those Easterners who are so eager to go west." This was during the 1850s, at the beginning of the Gold Rush, when people were heading for California by ship, wagon, horseback, or on foot.

"When they get there," the young man continued, "they can take the flatboats apart and use the wood for houses." He filled in the rest of his plan so cleverly that Thomas agreed to join him, even if it meant turning away from the sea.

The next morning, Thomas and his partner caught the stagecoach for Kansas, where they hoped to sell their flatboat wagons to Easterners crossing the Missouri River. As they traveled farther into the open country, Thomas began to enjoy it.

Later, when he saw vast stretches of prairie ahead, with the wind making waves through the grass, he felt as though he had almost gone back to sea.

At Westport Landing, Kansas, Thomas and his partner bought lumber and wagon wheels. Neither of them knew much about carpentry, but their design was simple—a box made of strong wooden planks resting on two long beams. The hardest part was attaching the wheels so that they could turn freely without coming loose. Thomas tried to do it with bits of rope, which didn't work.

"Why don't we just give people four wheels," his partner said impatiently, "and let them figure it out?"

Then along came someone from Charleston, South Carolina, who showed them how to carve wooden axles for the wheels. Soon the job was done, and their first flatboat wagon was ready to sell. They put up a sign by the river's edge and waited for customers. A few people stopped to look, but nobody wanted to buy. They lowered the price, and lowered it again. Still no sale.

"I like your idea," a man said, "but I just can't afford it. The prices for horses or mules are sky-high right now, and it would take at least two of them to pull that thing."

So Thomas and his partner reluctantly decided to go out of business. They would remove the wagon wheels, find a cargo, and carry it down to New Orleans, where they could sell the flatboat and Thomas could go back to sea.

At the very last minute, standing by the river with a brisk breeze blowing, Thomas had a better idea.

"We don't need horses or mules for this thing," the sailor said. "All we need to do is add a mast and a sail."

His partner was doubtful, but Thomas persuaded him to try it. With the last of their money, they bought an oak tree for a mast, a smaller one for the boom, and clean white canvas to make a sail. Then some rope for the rigging, stones for ballast, and the world's first windwagon was ready to go!

Thomas and his partner jumped aboard, hoisted the sail, and caught the breeze blowing west from the river. Once they were clear of town, the windwagon gained speed, and soon they were racing across the smooth, grassy prairie toward the setting sun. Thomas was so excited that he forgot about trying to steer the windwagon or slow it down. Straight as a seabird they flew with the wind, hour after hour, until finally they crashed into the purple foothills of the Rocky Mountains, more than a thousand miles west of their starting point. From there they decided to walk the rest of the way to California, and they never came back.

Sweet Betsey from Pike

Elizabeth Curry was the prettiest girl in Pike County, Missouri, though she didn't want to be. She wore long dresses, fancy shoes, and hair ribbons because she had to—going to school, going to church, visiting relatives in St. Louis or Columbia. Whenever she could get free for a while, even a few hours in the afternoon, she'd put on a pair of her brother's faded, castoff blue jeans, an old buckskin shirt, and her treasured Indian moccasins. Then she'd wrap a scarf around the golden glory of her hair, and try to sneak out of the house.

"Betsey!" her mother would wail. "Where are you going in those outlandish clothes? Whose horse are you riding? I don't know what's to become of you."

Betsey didn't know what was to become of herself either, but she usually found some excuse and slipped through the doorway before her mother could stop her. Outside she'd head for the hill behind her house, where she could gaze in all directions, or the livery stable where she was sometimes allowed to exercise horses. Today she felt like doing both—borrowing a horse, riding it to the top of her hill, choosing a new destination, and galloping away from town. But where to? That was always the problem.

Down at the livery stable Betsey got a surprise. Her best friend, Ike Henderson, was selling both of his horses.

"Goin' to California," Ike explained. "Goin' to buy a wagon and two yoke of oxen, and join the Gold Rush that everybody's talkin' about."

He was a big, awkward fellow, a few years older than Betsey, with a sweet disposition and something of the romantic in him, despite his serious expression.

"You're not really leaving without me, are you?" cried Betsey. "My father says it's only Fool's Gold, as like as not."

For nearly an hour she tried to talk Ike out of going, but his mind was made up. He had sold most of his belongings and was joining a wagon train tomorrow. Betsey finally said goodbye to him and went home, feeling miserable, avoiding her parents' anxious glances while she pondered what to do.

The next morning it was Betsey who surprised Ike, climbing aboard his wagon as he was about to hit the trail with the others.

"Don't ask," she said firmly. "I'm eighteen years old, and I'm going with you."

At first it was a great adventure for both of them, learning to drive the oxen, cooking their meals in the open, sleeping on opposite sides of the wagon or under the stars. Ike's old yellow dog slept too, his spotted hog stood guard all night, and his Shanghai rooster woke them at dawn.

After three or four weeks, however, they were getting tired of traveling. The wagon train creaked slowly along, day after day, and there was little to talk about except gold or the weather. Kansas was even flatter than Missouri—when Ike's yellow dog ran away, they could see the dust it raised for miles.

"Dog gone," said Ike, trying to make light of their loss.

Up through the Colorado foothills they toiled, into the Rocky Mountains, where Ike traded his rooster for a used guitar and some lessons. To pass the time away, he began writing a song:

"Did you ever hear of Sweet Betsey from Pike?
She crossed the wide prairies with her HUM-HUM Ike. . . ."

Betsey looked across the campfire at Ike, pulled off her sunbonnet, and shook out her thick golden hair.

"What's HUM-HUM?" she asked.

"Whatever you say it is," Ike replied, blushing.

So they were married near Salt Lake City, Utah, by a Mormon preacher, and Betsey continued the journey westward with her husband. After rafting across the wide Platte River, they had to drop out of the wagon train when they lost a wheel. They sold their four oxen to buy supplies.

"Ike," said Betsey, "we've already found something more precious than gold. Do we have to walk all the way to California?"

"No, Betsey, I guess not," her loving husband replied.

They settled near Las Vegas, Nevada, and started a livery stable, which prospered. A golden-haired daughter, born to them the following year, was the prettiest girl in Clark County, though she didn't want to be.

Sheepherder from Yale

Augustus Butterfield, known as "Buster," was the fastest runner at Yale University during the 1920s. He broke all records in the 100-yard dash, the quarter-mile, the half-mile, and the mile. He also took an overload of courses, studied five hours a day, and waited tables in the dining room to help pay for his education. In his junior year, Buster was sometimes so busy that he put on his track suit first thing in the morning and ran from one place to another until midnight. People wondered if he ever slept.

Buster was training to run the Boston Marathon, in late April, when suddenly he collapsed from exhaustion. His doctors told him that he should take a year off, go out West, and build up his health. So Buster packed his trunk, said "so long" to Yale, and went home for a week. Then he took the train to Arizona, sleeping most of the way. He got off at a station called Happy Valley, where the air was clear and nobody had ever heard of a track star in those days.

"Wow!" Buster exclaimed. He stood on the deserted railroad platform, took a deep breath, and looked around him. Early morning sunlight made things gleam. At first he thought the valley was covered with white flowers, or maybe cotton, but then he realized that he was seeing sheep—thousands of them—all moving slowly in waves as they nibbled the tender spring grass. Here and there a person could be seen, or a sheepdog running excitedly in big circles around one of the herds, but nobody paid any attention to Buster until a wagon approached. The driver was a heavy, sun-bronzed old fellow with a brown-and-white collie riding beside him.

"You lookin' for work?" he asked.

Buster said yes, and the man explained that he owned most of the sheep in Happy Valley. He had eight sheepherders working for him, but now he needed one more—someone who could take charge of a couple of thousand of the woolly white animals, keep them together, and find any that got lost. The pay would be a dollar a day plus room and board.

"I'll take it," said Buster. "It sounds like just the sort of thing I need to do."

They rode in the wagon to an adobe bunkhouse, where Buster opened his trunk and put on his track suit—long white shorts, a sleeveless white jersey that had a big blue "Y" on the front, and black running shoes with spikes. The sheep owner had never seen an outfit like that before, and it didn't seem very practical to him, but he chuckled to himself and said nothing about it.

As they drove through the valley, Buster noticed how the grazing sheep were marked with patches of colored dye on their left sides—some red, some yellow, some green, some blue. The wagon stopped in the middle of a herd with blue markings.

"Just keep these blue ones together," the sheep owner said. "Don't let them get mixed with any other color. And be sure you round up the lambs."

Now this was meant as a joke. Anyone who knew anything about sheep could see that there were no lambs in the herd, nothing but full-grown males and females. Lambs would not be born until May or June, so there was no rounding-up to do now. But the new sheepherder, Buster, didn't get the joke—because his knowledge of lambs was limited to a song he had heard at Yale.

Buster tried his best to do two different things at once—keep the herd together and go after the ones that strayed—and he wished that he had the help of an experienced sheepdog. Another sheepherder brought him food and water at lunch time, but Buster was too busy to eat or drink. He ran and ran and ran. At sundown he had his herd of blue-marked sheep all rounded up and waiting when the sheep owner came back in the wagon.

"So how many lambs did you find?" asked the sheep owner, with a smile.

"Fifty-two," Buster replied proudly. "I made a pen for them over there in the bushes."

The sheep owner was startled—he went quickly to look. In Buster's pen he counted forty-seven of Arizona's finest jackrabbits and five gray cottontails—all bouncing and hopping nervously around. He laughed for quite a while. After that he didn't try to play a joke on Buster Butterfield again.

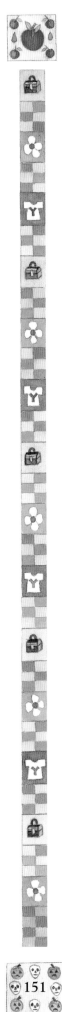

Calamity Jane

Martha Jane Canary was born in Iowa or Missouri or Wyoming between 1850 and 1860—nobody seems to know exactly where or when. Her mother's identity is also a mystery. Her father may have been a soldier who died young or left her behind at an army camp out West. In any event, Jane grew up among soldiers and their wives. From the women she learned how to look after herself and to care for the sick and wounded. From the men she learned how to ride, shoot, rope a horse, and fight with her knife or her fists.

When she arrived in Deadwood, South Dakota, as a young woman, Jane was tall, dark-haired, almost pretty, very independent, smart about some things, and fully capable of holding her own with just about anybody she ran into. She got a job working for a doctor, and she was reasonably content. Then she met James Butler Hickok, a big, handsome, adventurous man who went by the name of "Wild Bill." He was her equal in every way, and she was his. In a more settled time and place, the two of them might have fallen in love and lived happily ever after. But in the raw, violent frontier town of Deadwood, this was impossible. Every day, sometimes more than once, Bill had to prove how fearless he was. And so did Jane. Their tender feelings rarely showed. Instead of becoming sweethearts they became friends, but also competitors—testing their skills against each other, to see who could ride faster, drink more, yell louder, or hit a smaller target with a Colt .45? Sometimes they would roam the streets of Deadwood together, both dressed in buckskins and boots, carrying guns, looking for trouble and usually finding it.

One night in 1876, while Jane was visiting some friends, Bill went off to play cards with his pals at a new saloon. The game was poker, and Bill had pretty good luck. But he paid too much attention to his cards and didn't notice who was standing nearby. Just as Bill was about to scoop up the pot, a man he hardly knew came up behind him and shot him in the head. Why? Maybe because of something that had happened years before, when Bill was a U.S. Marshal in Kansas. There's no way to tell. But the cards that Hickok held when he died, two aces and two eights, have since been known as "the dead man's hand."

That was the biggest calamity in Jane's unhappy life—at least the biggest we know of. When she got back to town and heard about Bill's death, she went crazy with rage. She would have killed the murderer, if she could have found him, but the man disappeared. There was a lengthy funeral where Jane cried openly with dozens of Bill's friends and admirers. At the cemetery, she rubbed a little prairie dust into the newly-cut letters of Hickok's name on the gravestone, so that he might feel more at home there. She wanted to be buried next to him, but no matter how hard she tried, no matter how recklessly she lived, it took her nearly twenty-seven years to get there.

Jane did her level best to become as wild as Bill Hickok had been—maybe wilder. She never refused a bet, a challenge, a dare. She hunted with army scouts, herded cattle with cowboys, chased outlaws with posses. To make ends meet, she sometimes worked in carnivals doing trick shots with rifle or pistols, and she appeared as "CALAMITY JANE" in Wild West shows as far East as Buffalo, New York. She earned money when she could and spent it wherever she happened to be. But her heart was back in Deadwood, South Dakota, and she always returned there. Often she visited Bill Hickok's grave, where souvenir hunters had chipped away bits of the gravestone until it made her feel all the worse to see it.

As she grew older, Jane began to show her fearlessness in a different way. She frequently volunteered to nurse people suffering from smallpox and other contagious diseases. In those days, and those places, doctors and trained nurses were rare; hospitals were nonexistent. Somehow, this rough and reckless woman could be gentle and sure

of herself with the sick. So Jane was always welcome, in spite of her reputation for hard living. This went on until her courage caught up with her, and she died of an infection when she was about fifty years old.

Calamity Jane was buried beside Bill Hickok, where she wanted to be, and the words that people spoke at her funeral were full of fond memories of the two of them.

Other Tales of Colorful Characters

Elizabeth McCourt was known as "Baby Doe" because of her big brown eyes and innocent air. She married an older man named Horace Tabor who had made tons of money out of mining in Colorado. He bought her a $90,000 diamond necklace for a wedding present and much else besides, but his luck ran out later, and all he left her when he died was a mine that most people considered worthless. Baby Doe had two children to raise, however, and no diamonds left, so she decided to give it a try. Year after year she scratched a little gold dust from the leavings heaped up beside the mine shaft. Finally even that was gone, and she died penniless at age seventy-five.

Baby Doe's husband, Horace Tabor, was the kind of fellow who loved to spend it while he had it. For instance, when he found that Denver needed a new opera house, Tabor decided to create and give the city "a matchless specimen of modern architecture," vintage 1881. He gathered pictures of similar buildings from the Eastern cities and Europe, hiring a local architect to combine all of the best features into a design that was hard to appreciate and harder to build. But Tabor was extremely pleased with the results, except for one thing—a painting of William Shakespeare in the lobby. "What has he ever done for Colorado?" Tabor demanded. "Take it down and put my picture up there."

An Ohio office worker quit his job and headed west in the 1890s, because he had heard about people finding gold and hoped there might be some left for him. He was so busy talking with his wife as they bounced along in the wagon that he didn't pay much attention to his three children playing games with a bucketful of shiny pebbles in the back. By the time he realized that the pebbles contained gold only one or two remained, and his children couldn't remember where they had found them along the way. The original source of these pebbles, wherever it might have been, is still known as the "Blue Bucket Mine."

Like many other people, Thea Foss created her own business because she had to make a living and she couldn't find a job. Starting with a leaky rowboat that someone had abandoned near Tacoma, Washington, Thea ran errands for ships anchored in Puget Sound while they waited for space at the docks. She was so hard-working and dependable that she soon had plenty of customers, and her business prospered in the man's world of the waterfront. She ended up as owner of the Foss Tug Company—a dynamic, successful woman on whose life the rollicking "Tugboat Annie" movies were loosely based.

Two easy-going young brothers, Pablo and Pedro, were hired by a nervous old man to deliver a spirited horse to his ranch near Taos, New Mexico. "Now remember," the rancher said, "this here's a dangerous, bad-tempered creature, and I want you to lead him on foot. Promise me that neither of you boys will let the other ride this horse." Pedro and Pablo agreed but the day was hot, the dusty road stretched endlessly ahead of them, and the horse seemed good-natured. After a while Pablo asked Pedro, "What if we both rode the horse at the same time? That way, neither of us would be letting the other do it." Pedro agreed and up they sprang, riding bareback. The horse galloped along happily as he showed off his speed. They reached Taos much earlier than expected, so all three took a *siesta* before approaching the old man's ranch.

Tam came to America from Vietnam with her parents, and the family was happy at first. Later her mother died, her father remarried, a sister named Cam was born, and Tam's happiness gradually ended. Her stepmother was cruel to her, always favoring the lazy Cam, while Tam had to wear the same clothes to school every day and clean the house afterwards. When Tam was old enough to marry, a wonderful goddess introduced her to a princely young man who truly appreciated her goodness and beauty. Killed by her jealous stepmother just as she was soaring to new heights of happiness, Tam came back to life and joyfully reclaimed her prince, thanks again to the goddess.

Emmeline Labiche grew up in French-speaking Canada and got engaged to her childhood sweetheart, Louis Arceneaux, when she was sixteen. Before they could be married, however, disaster struck their village—British troops came to move them out of homes that were wanted for English-speaking colonists. In the confusion, Louis was wounded and left behind, while Emmeline and her mother were transported to Maryland. Later the Labiche family moved to Louisiana, where the ever-faithful Emmeline discovered Louis, alive and well, about to marry another woman. Emmeline died of a broken heart, but was immortalized as Longfellow's "Evangeline."

Rose Ann McCoy never traveled far from home, a cabin overlooking the creek that separates Kentucky from West Virginia. When it came time to marry, there were few men to choose from, and the one who caught her eye, Johnse Hatfield, had two strikes against him—he was already married, and the Hatfields were involved in a bitter feud with the McCoys. But Rose Ann pursued Johnse anyway, and the conflict deepened between the two families. After Johnse's wife was hit by a stray bullet, he met Rose Ann's cousin Nancy, a sensible girl who steered him skillfully through courtship and marriage, thus helping to end the feud.

Sweethearts and other colorful characters are often found in folk tales from particular localities. For example, see Harold Thompson's *Body Boots & Britches* for upstate New York, Cohen and Dillingham's *Humor of the Old Southwest*, Marie Campbell's *Tales from the Cloud Walking Country*, and B. A. Botkin's *Sidewalks of America*.

INCREDIBLE ANIMALS

Br'er Rabbit and Br'er Fox

Back in the days when small animals roamed freely through the woods and fields of rural Georgia, they were usually peaceable. Rabbits, squirrels, chipmunks, raccoons, possums, and other creatures thought of themselves as one big family. They called each other "Brother" and "Sister" when they happened to meet while looking for food in the underbrush or getting a drink of water at the creek. Br'er Rabbit might disagree with Br'er Possum about something, or Sis' Squirrel might scold her youngsters, or several Raccoons might try to take a meal away from Crows. But most of the time, there were no serious quarrels.

This all changed as families of red foxes moved down into Georgia from Virginia and the Carolinas to get away from angry farmers, who considered them a great nuisance. Georgia was still wide open, with miles of meadows and pine woods where foxes could hunt to their hearts' content. Georgia's clay soil was perfect for digging burrows that were snug and easy to defend. So the red foxes quickly adapted to their new environment and forced other animals to change. Since foxes preferred to hunt at night, raccoons and possums stayed hidden then and did their own hunting during the daytime. Rabbits bunched together in huge colonies that foxes hesitated to attack. Chipmunks and squirrels shifted their nests from the ground into the trees, building new homes high among the swaying boughs where no fox could climb. Crows and other birds served as lookouts, yelling warnings when a fox showed up. Every animal did something to help.

Every animal, that is, except one—a small, soft-nosed rabbit with big floppy ears

and a quick, active mind. He called himself "Br'er Rabbit," like thousands of rabbits in that part of Georgia, but he differed from the others. This particular Br'er Rabbit was proud, self-confident, and unusually bright. He wasn't about to run from any number of foxes, and he refused to huddle with the rest of the rabbits in crowded, frightened communities. Br'er Rabbit had his own comfortable home, deep inside an enormous thicket of thorny wild roses, with delicious perfume surrounding him, and the gentle humming of bees. He was almost certain that foxes couldn't get at him

there, but he wanted to be one hundred percent sure. So he added to his natural defenses with sharp-pointed quills given to him by Br'er Porcupine, some pungent musk from Br'er Skunk, and other tricks and surprises he kept to himself.

Though his life seemed pleasant and safe, Br'er Rabbit did have a problem or two. He wasn't quite as smart as he thought he was, so he stumbled into trouble at times. And because he didn't socialize much with other animals, he didn't always get to hear the news. For example, Br'er Rabbit wasn't aware that a new enemy had moved into the forest nearby. This was a fox, not an ordinary red fox, but a sly old fellow with gray fur, a gray top hat, and a shiny pair of nose glasses he had found somewhere else. He looked like a city slicker, out of place in the country, and that's what he was.

He called himself "Br'er Fox," but the other animals were not so sure that he deserved such a familiar name. Living by his wits, which had been sharpened with experience, he managed to do very well. The country life was not exciting for Br'er Fox, however, so when he heard that his new neighbors included a solitary rabbit more clever than most, he was very interested. At last, the possibility of a worthy opponent! Br'er Fox spent the afternoon making special preparations, then took a long snooze in his burrow while he waited for Br'er Rabbit to appear.

Awakened by the pit-pat, pittery-pat of footsteps, Br'er Fox peeked out as Br'er Rabbit hopped lightly along a path that zig-zagged through the woods from his home to his favorite

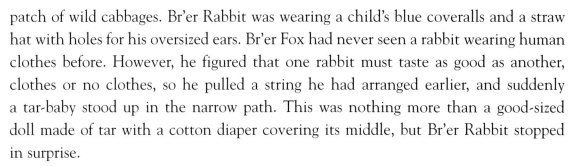

patch of wild cabbages. Br'er Rabbit was wearing a child's blue coveralls and a straw hat with holes for his oversized ears. Br'er Fox had never seen a rabbit wearing human clothes before. However, he figured that one rabbit must taste as good as another, clothes or no clothes, so he pulled a string he had arranged earlier, and suddenly a tar-baby stood up in the narrow path. This was nothing more than a good-sized doll made of tar with a cotton diaper covering its middle, but Br'er Rabbit stopped in surprise.

"What do you want?" he asked.

Br'er Fox chuckled in the bushes, for he knew what he wanted, while the tar-baby was silent.

"Do you want something?" Br'er Rabbit persisted. "Otherwise, stand aside, and let me pass."

The tar-baby remained silent.

"I'll just be on my way, then," Br'er Rabbit continued.

He tried to squeeze past the tar-baby without touching it, but the path was too narrow. Br'er Fox, still hiding, pulled his string again, and the tar-baby fell heavily against Br'er Rabbit, getting sticky black tar all over his blue coveralls.

"Where are you going?" Br'er Rabbit cried. "Watch what you're doing!"

He moved this way and that, but the tar-baby swung around and remained close to him, so that Br'er Rabbit got smeared with more and more of the sticky tar, whichever way he turned. His blue coveralls were now ruined, and the brim of his straw hat was also smeared with tar. Angrily, Br'er Rabbit pushed against the tar-baby with both front paws to move him out of the way. But he only got stuck deeper.

"I'll show him," Br'er Rabbit thought, and launched a mighty kick at the tar-baby with his strong back legs. But now his back paws got stuck in the tar as well, and he fell to the ground, rolling over and struggling to get up. He couldn't do it. The harder he tried, the worse he did. Finally he lay on the ground, panting, exhausted, looking more like a tar-baby than the tar-baby itself. Only then did Br'er Fox emerge from the bushes, bowing and smirking at his helpless captive.

"Good afternoon, Brother Rabbit," he said silkily. "How nice of you to accept my invitation for dinner."

As upset as he was, Br'er Rabbit instantly sensed danger, and started thinking of how to get away.

"Just being neighborly, Brother Fox," he replied, "just being neighborly. But first I'll hop along home, clean myself up, and be back with you directly."

"No need, Brother," said Br'er Fox. "It's going to be a real casual meal. Since you have trouble walking, I'll pull you along by the ears."

That turned out to be quite uncomfortable for Br'er Rabbit, as Br'er Fox hauled him through the bushes towards his burrow, but there was no use in complaining now.

"Anything you say, Brother Fox," said Br'er Rabbit, "anything you say is fine with me, but please—"

He paused, and Br'er Fox waited politely.

"Please," Br'er Rabbit went on, "do not throw me into that awful briar patch, over there to your left."

Br'er Fox, still unfamiliar with much of country life, didn't see how getting thrown into a briar patch could be more painful than getting cooked for rabbit stew. But he had a cruel streak in his nature, like many foxes, and the idea of this tar-streaked rabbit squirming and suffering rather pleased him.

"Are you sure you wouldn't like me to throw you in there, tar and all?" he asked.

"Abso-tee-totally positive," Br'er Rabbit replied. "I can't think of anything worse."

Hearing that, Br'er Fox swung Br'er Rabbit back and forth several times, then hurled him through the air to the middle of the briar patch, where he disappeared among roses and thorns.

"Ouch! Ouch!" cried Br'er Rabbit, as he quickly activated his secret defenses. "Please come and save me, Mr. Fox!"

Br'er Fox found what seemed to be an entrance and plunged forward, only to stop short as porcupine quills hit him in the nose and raked him on the sides. Skunk's musk enveloped him with its clinging aroma. Thorns tore at him, whichever way he moved, and something like a snake hissed, then struck at his unprotected belly. Ants swarmed up his legs. Even the bees that had been buzzing in the background rose to sting him. When he finally succeeded in turning around, he crawled painfully out of the briar patch, leaving his gray hat and his eyeglasses behind as he ran yelping through the woods.

A few minutes later, when the bees had resumed their pleasant humming, Br'er Rabbit hopped down to the creek, where some of the other animals were gathered.

"What kind of critter was that?" Sis' Possum asked, as she helped Br'er Rabbit to clean himself up.

"Some kind of fox, maybe, or a coyote," he replied.

"Whatever," she continued. "It was right neighborly of you to run him out of here, and we thank you kindly."

Compair Bouki and the Monkeys

Many years ago, when Louisiana still belonged to France, an old black man lived by himself among the bayous—those long bays of water that reach back into the swamps. He liked to eat, and he bragged to his neighbors that he could catch fish with his bare hands, or find melons growing wild, or make a tasty drink from the bark of the live oak tree.

But he also said things that made no sense to them—for example, he claimed that the trees surrounding his house were full of monkeys. His neighbors knew there weren't any monkeys in the bayou country, so they called him "Compair Bouki," and told stories that did not flatter him. *"Compair"* means "fellow" or "man" in French. *"Bouki"* is an African name for the hyena, an animal easily deceived, although it looks smart enough at first glance.

The story about Compair Bouki and the monkeys made his neighbors laugh the most. Came a day, they said, when he could find nothing to eat. It didn't occur to him to ask anyone for help. Instead he thought of a plan to get some food. First he gathered wood and built a cooking fire near his house. When it was hot, he filled his largest pot with water, and put it on to boil. In a few minutes, steam was rising from the pot. Then Compair Bouki marched around his yard, beating a drum and shouting:

"Sam-bombel! Sam-bombel tum!

Sam-bombel! Sam-bombel dum!"

His words didn't mean anything—he made them up because he wanted to attract the attention of the monkeys. Sure enough, some of the younger monkeys heard

Compair Bouki shouting about food. They crept closer through the trees, and saw his big pot steaming on the fire. Being hungry themselves, they assumed he had something good to eat. They sang this song:

"Molési cherguinet, chourvan!

Chéguillé, chourvan!"

Listening to the monkeys singing, Compair Bouki thought he heard French words for vegetables and stew. He chuckled to himself—the monkeys must be falling for his trick! Five or six of them were peeking from the trees, and he called to them:

"I am going to climb into the pot, and make myself part of the stew. But I don't want to stay there too long. When I say, 'I am cooked,' you must reach in right away and pull me out. Do you agree?"

The young monkeys nodded their heads, and gathered around the pot. Compair Bouki jumped in, but the water was boiling hot, so he cried "I am cooked" almost immediately, and the monkeys pulled him out.

Compair Bouki said, "Now it's your turn—you climb into the pot, and when you say you are cooked, I will pull you out."

As soon as the monkeys were in the pot, Compair Bouki put a heavy lid on top, trapping them inside.

"We are cooked! We are cooked!" they cried, but Compair Bouki shouted back at them: "No, not yet! If you were truly cooked, you could not say so!"

Compair Bouki went into his house to set the table for lunch. While he was inside, three older monkeys came quickly out of the woods, lifted the lid from the pot, and helped their younger relatives to escape.

Not realizing what had happened, Compair Bouki served himself a bowl of hot water from the pot. Believing this to be monkey stew, he found it very tasty! He spooned up more and more until the pot was almost empty, and he fell asleep. But when he awoke the next morning, he was hungrier than ever, so he decided to play his trick again. When the pot was boiling, he turned toward the trees and shouted:

"Sam-bombel! Sam-bombel tum!

Sam-bombel! Sam-bombel dum!"

Sure enough, eight or nine monkeys came out of the woods and listened to him:

"When I say, 'I am cooked' you must reach in right away and pull me out. Do you agree?"

The monkeys nodded. So Compair Bouki climbed into the pot of boiling water, as before, and almost immediately he yelled, "I am cooked!" But this time the monkeys did not help.

"If you were truly cooked," the oldest monkey responded, "you could not say so."

Two-Toe Tom, the Giant Alligator

Two-Toe Tom was an alligator that lived in the marshes near Montgomery, Alabama. How did he get his name? Some folks said he had lost two of his toes in a fight, or a trap. Others thought maybe he had only two toes left. But most folks never got close enough to find out. Instead, they told stories about Tom—he can climb trees like a snake, he can dig tunnels in the mud, from one pond to the next, he can disappear if you blink your eye. And when anything upset them, they blamed it on him—Tom ate six of my chickens, Tom scared my kids, Tom stole my brand-new mule. Before long, Two-Toe Tom was known as the biggest, ugliest, smartest, fastest-moving alligator in all of Tallapoosa County. Hardly anybody wanted to meet him face to face.

But then things changed, as they usually do. Down in Florida, near the Everglades, a man named "Gator" Johnson heard about Two-Toe Tom. Gator was a professional hunter. For a price, he would kill or capture any animal that preyed on farmers and their livestock. He specialized in alligators. His barn was full of huge jawbones, with rows of teeth as sharp as bucksaws, and he had scars on his arms and legs where some of those teeth had bitten him. However, the alligators in that part of Florida were ten feet long at most, including their tails. Gator was ready to tackle a really big one, so he packed his wagon with supplies and equipment, and headed north.

"Two-Toe Tom," he said to himself as he drove along. "Two

tons, more likely. Fourteen foot if he's an inch! I just can't wait to get my hands on that critter."

Gator crossed the border into Alabama and found his way to Tallapoosa County. Everyone he met had heard of Two-Toe Tom, and a few people claimed to have seen him, but no one knew exactly where he could be found. The farms were mostly like islands surrounded by marshland, full of shallow ponds, and Tom seemed to live in all of these places.

But that didn't bother Gator Johnson one bit. He had to start somewhere, so he set up his camp near the edge of the biggest pond, fed his mules, and shucked a few ears of corn for himself. While they were cooking, he unloaded his flat-bottomed boat from the wagon and dragged it toward the water. Suddenly he stopped. He could feel something stirring. Then, in the stillness of the pond, an enormous snout appeared just above the surface, and a big eye glared at him. Gator was scared for a moment, then tremendously excited.

"Fourteen foot, maybe fifteen!" he shouted. "My oh my, ain't you a beauty!"

Two-Toe Tom had not been described as a beauty before. He was surprised and pleased. Instead of grabbing Gator for a quick meal, which he could easily have done, Tom remained still, savoring the moment, almost dozing off. His eyes actually closed. But he snapped them open again to see that Gator had run over to the wagon for something. Tom didn't wait to find out what it might be. Instead he slid through the water to the shore, caught Gator's boat in his great jaws, and crunched it like a fried tomato sandwich. When Gator came running back, all that remained to be seen were a few scraps of wood floating on the surface of the pond, and a pair of electrical wires stretching out toward the middle. Toe-Two Tom was gone.

"That's all right," said Gator. "That's just fine." He was carrying a miner's box called a detonator. When he set it down and pushed the plunger on top, the dynamite he had hidden on his boat exploded somewhere out in the depths of the pond. More pieces of wood flew up into the air, along with bones and other things that had rested in the mud for a long time. But no sign of alligators.

For several weeks, Gator Johnson stayed in Tallapoosa County, Alabama, looking around, moving from one pond to another, without finding any trace of old Tom.

"Guess I got him," Gator told the farmers.

"Guess you did," the farmers agreed. They couldn't afford to pay him cash, they said, but they loaded up Gator's wagon with corn and other vegetables, and gave him an extra mule. As he drove home to Florida he never looked back, so he didn't see the giant alligator coming happily behind him down the dusty road, grinning like a lovesick hound that has found its true master at last.

Goat Sees Red

Hector Hardscrabble worked in a tire and rubber factory near Philadelphia. All day long he packed new automobile tires into big cardboard cartons to be shipped to garages and gas stations around the country. It was an easy job that left him plenty of time for his own thoughts, but he was ready for a change. What he really wanted was to be a farmer, as his father had been. During his lunch hour, while other workers were talking or resting, Hector would look at the "Farms for Sale" advertisements in the newspapers, and think about having a place of his own.

This was during the 1930s, when times were hard for most people. Farm prices were dropping lower and lower, but Hector didn't have much money saved up, so he kept on reading the ads until finally he found a farm listed for less than two thousand dollars. It had a house, a barn, some woods, and nearly eighty acres of tillable land.

After work, Hector made a telephone call to find out more about the place. Then he hurried home to tell his wife, Harriet.

"What's the catch?" was her first question.

"Well, it's pretty far from here," Hector replied. "About halfway between Philadelphia and Scranton. Back up in the hills, kind of."

"Up in the mountains, you mean. What else?"

"Well, the soil is probably kind of stony."

"And?" Harriet demanded.

"And there seems to be a railroad track running right through the middle of it.

But the place comes with some livestock," Hector added hastily. "Four dozen hens, and a rooster, and two cows, and a goat. We could make a living there."

Harriet said nothing more for the moment. She was a farmer's daughter herself, and she knew how hard it was for two people to make a living even on the best of farms. But she also knew her husband—Hector had his heart set on getting back to the land. She understood his feeling, so she talked the whole thing over with him that night, and finally they agreed to try it. Hector gave her a big hug.

"Honey, you'll never regret this," he assured her. "If anybody can make a go of the place, it's us."

"You may just be right," Harriet replied. "You're the stubbornest guy I ever heard of, and you know the way I can make ends meet, so we do have a chance, at least."

After the first month or two, Hector and Harriet both felt that they were doing the right thing. The house was small but cozy, and freshly painted. The barn looked almost new. The chickens laid plenty of eggs, big tan ones with brown speckles, and Harriet soon had a steady flow of customers from the little town nearby—people who would rather not buy their eggs in a store. Also, the land was not quite so stony and barren as she had feared. Hector plowed three large fields and planted a crop of "eating" corn in them. At night he read "how to" booklets about new techniques of farming from the state agricultural office. Harriet was glad to see him looking so happy.

Hector worked six days a week and rarely complained. On the seventh day, however, he liked to rest and go to church with Harriet. He usually wore a red silk shirt that she had given him for his birthday. It was his way of saying that going to church meant something special to him.

One Saturday afternoon in September, Harriet carefully washed Hector's red  shirt and hung it outdoors so that it would be dry the next day. A cool breeze snapped the wet cloth, making the shirt wave back and forth like a red flag. Soon it caught the attention of the big yellow-eyed goat that had lived on the farm for years. This animal was self-satisfied, more or less useless, and a little bit mysterious to Hector, who hadn't ever owned a goat before.

The goat evidently liked red things better than anything else in the world—apples, the covers of Sears catalogs, ketchup bottles, tin cans, whatever he happened to find. He looked at things, he picked them up, they disappeared. Did he eat them or just bury them? Hector was never sure.

But this time, as he looked out the kitchen window, Hector actually saw the goat rear up on his hind legs, grab the red shirt in his teeth, and yank it down from the wash line, clothespins and all. Then the goat started swallowing one sleeve of his shirt! Hector put down the fried egg sandwich he was eating and ran out of the house.

"Let go of my red shirt, you stupid cuss!" he shouted. But the goat paid no attention and continued to swallow the shirt, as though he had never tasted anything half so good.

"Let go, let go!" Hector grabbed the end of the other sleeve before it vanished, and tried not to tear his shirt as he pulled. But this goat was the stubbornest of the stubborn—he dug in his feet, he kept on swallowing, and soon there wasn't anything to be seen of Hector's, except for one or two red threads caught between the goat's front teeth.

Harriet came running from the chicken house when she heard the fuss.

"Hector, it's all right," she said. "I've got some extra money saved up now, from the eggs. I'll buy you another red shirt."

But for Hector it wasn't all right. He wanted his own shirt back, period. If he couldn't have it, this blankety-blank goat wasn't going to enjoy it either! Hector cut a piece of rope from the clothesline, put a loop of it around the goat's neck, and started dragging him across the farmyard. Naturally the goat dug in all four of his feet, but Hector was strong and angry, so the two of them moved slowly off in the general direction of the woods.

"Hector Hardscrabble," his wife cried. "Whatever are you doing? You're not going to hang that poor animal?"

"Hanging's too good for him," Hector yelled back. "I'm going to teach him something he'll never forget—if he lives long enough to remember it."

Harriet followed at a distance,

168

as Hector dragged the reluctant goat through the woods to the single railroad track that cut across the middle of their farm. A train whistle sounded in the distance— they were just in time for the afternoon freight. Using his rope, Hector quickly tied the goat across the tracks where the train would be sure to hit him.

"Oh, Hector, you can't do this," Harriet protested, but Hector wasn't about to stop now.

"Teach him something he'll never forget," Hector repeated, panting with effort. "I can be stubborn too."

He waited until the train was getting close, then turned his back on the goat and walked away.

"Hector?" Harriet pleaded.

"Nope," said Hector. "My mind's made up."

Meanwhile the goat—seeing the train coming at him—quickly coughed up most of Hector's red shirt. He waved his head back and forth as hard as he could. The man driving the train leaned out and saw something that looked like a flag—red for danger—on the tracks ahead. So he slammed on the brakes and the train squealed to a stop, just inches away from the goat.

Hector looked back, saw what was going on, and ran to get his shirt before anything else could happen to it.

"This your goat?" asked the train driver.

"Yes, but I've been thinking about getting rid of him," Hector replied.

"I can see that," the man said. "Would you be interested in getting rid of him a different way?"

"How do you mean?" said Hector cautiously.

"Fact is, I've always wanted to have a goat like that for a pet," the man explained. "I couldn't pay you any money, but maybe I could trade you something for him. How about—how about this pair of red suspenders I'm wearing?"

Hector looked at the red suspenders, and so did the goat. Hector thought those suspenders would go real well with his favorite red shirt, but he didn't know what the goat was thinking.

There was a long moment of silence, while steam hissed gently from the engine of the train. Then the goat turned towards him, and Hector looked straight into the animal's deep, fearless yellow eyes. Something happened.

"I don't know," said Hector. "How about I trade you this red shirt for the suspenders, and I keep the goat?"

"All right by me," the train driver said. "I sure do like that shirt."

"I like it myself," said Hector. "But I'm thinking that maybe I like it a bit too much."

So he gave the red shirt to the train driver, put on his new suspenders, picked up the rope, and led his goat home to the farmyard, where his loving wife stood beside the clothesline, hanging up a clean white shirt for him to wear to church.

Gollywhopper's Eggs

In the early days of this country, farmers had to grow or make most of what they needed, because there weren't many places to buy things, and they didn't have much money to spend. Some depended on peddlers, who walked from one farm to the next, carrying heavy packs of useful items for sale, such as pots and pans, buttons, hair ribbons, shoelaces, books, and small tools. Most of these peddlers were honest, hardworking men who eventually saved up enough money to open a store or quit peddling because they got worn out.

But one peddler in New England, a big curly-haired fellow by the name of Wily Swift, thought of an easier way to make money. Instead of selling people things they really needed, at fair prices, he sold them gollywhopper's eggs for five dollars apiece. Of course five dollars was a great deal of money in those days, but Wily was a clever salesman. He would talk for a while before he opened up his pack and let people see what a gollywhopper egg looked like. Then he would slowly bring out this brown, hairy "egg" about the size of a football.

"Why, that's the ugliest thing I ever did see," a farmer's wife might complain.

"Yes ma'am, it surely is," Wily would reply. "But you're not going to buy this egg for its looks. Remember what's inside, and what it can do for you."

Woman or man, young or old, Wily Swift would always tell them the following story:

"Many years ago, a New England sea captain discovered gollywhoppers on an uncharted island in the Pacific Ocean. These gollywhoppers are huge, wonderful birds

171

with clean white feathers—whiter than snow. They build their nests in palm trees, lay their eggs one by one, and leave them alone. Their eggs take several years to hatch. I happen to own four of them. I can't tell you exactly when this one will hatch, but it surely is worth waiting for! The lucky person who owns a gollywhopper will bless the day they bought it and marvel at the low price, for this is truly a marvelous bird."

"What's so marvelous about it?" someone would ask.

"Well, first of all, the gollywhopper eats almost nothing. Then it can do more work in a day than a hired hand could do in a week—for instance, pulling out tree

stumps, plowing with its beak, or harvesting a crop. It can pick apples faster than you can see. It can milk your cow, paint your barn, or guard your chickens from foxes and possums. In fact, there's only one thing a gollywhopper can't do, and I want to be honest with you about that."

"What can't it do?" the person would ask.

"It just can't seem to stop working," Wily Swift would reply. "If you tell it to stop, or even ask it nicely, the gollywhopper will get upset and run away. So maybe you better think twice about paying me five dollars for this egg."

"No, I don't mind that," the person would say. "There's always plenty of things to do around here."

"Well, that's all right then," Wily would continue. "Here's your egg. Just keep it in a nice warm place, on a bit of straw."

And then the farmer or the farmer's wife would slowly count out five dollars in small coins, and Wily would thank them and leave soon after.

This went on for five or six years. Wily Swift sold at least a hundred gollywhopper eggs to people all over New England, before anyone suspected the truth. He made enough money to buy himself a shiny new wagon and a good bay horse, and to put some money aside.

Then one summer day in 1836, Wily Swift drove up a rocky lane near Amherst, Massachusetts, to the farm of Alice Robinson, a pretty woman who had bought an egg from him three years before. Her sister, a sailor's wife, was visiting from New Bedford.

"Has your egg hatched yet?" Wily asked pleasantly. "Should be due just about any time now."

Alice said no, the egg hadn't hatched, and her sister asked what egg she was talking about. So the gollywhopper egg was produced from its cozy box of straw, trimmed with scraps of blue calico, and Alice's sister immediately recognized what it was—an ordinary coconut—but she said nothing at the moment. Looking at Wily Swift with a gleam in her eye, she suggested that he stay for supper. Alice liked the idea too. She kindly offered to wash and iron Wily's clothes as well, since he had told her he was a traveling man with nobody to look after him.

"Why that's mighty nice of you," said Wily. "And if I could sleep in your barn tonight, I'd be off in the morning before you knew it."

The three of them had a jolly meal together. Then Wily complimented Alice on her cooking and said good night. He left his clothes neatly piled outside the barn door, so that she could launder them. Then he climbed up to the hayloft, chuckled to himself, and fell sound asleep.

As Alice Robinson was washing Wily's clothes, her sister explained to her how she had been cheated by this good-looking peddler. Alice was upset, of course, and disappointed, but her sister had a plan for getting even.

About four o'clock the next morning, Wily was awakened by loud noises—his horse whinnying, and women screaming. He climbed down the rickety ladder from the hayloft as quickly as he could, but then realized he had no clothes to put on. So he stopped just inside the barn door, stuck his head out, and hollered towards the house.

"What's wrong?"

"Oh, Mr. Swift," Alice called back to him, "what a terrible night. How did you sleep through it all?"

"Sleep through what?" Wily demanded.

"Why, the gollywhopper hatched out around midnight, just as we were going to sleep. You never saw such a commotion! Before I could say anything, that gollywhopper washed all of the supper dishes including the pots and pans. Then he swept the kitchen floor. Then he ironed your clothes, faster than you could see him move. Then he dusted the whole house from top to bottom—it was wonderful, just like you promised, the whole place clean in less than an hour. Then I forgot—I asked him to stop! He rushed out, hitched your horse to that fine new wagon of yours, and went off down the lane. My sister's trying to catch him."

"What did this gollywhopper look like?" Wily said slowly.

"Why, just like you told me—feathers all over, white as snow. I wonder where he's got to?"

"I don't know," said Wily, "but I doubt if we'll ever see him again."

"Does that mean I get my money back?" asked Alice. "Just having a gollywhopper for a few hours doesn't seem like it's worth five dollars."

"Money cheerfully refunded," Wily said, not sounding very cheerful. He had kept all of his money in a secret compartment under the seat of his wagon, and there was no telling where it might be now. Then he thought of something else.

"What about my clothes?" he asked.

"Why, that gollywhopper took them with him, I do believe," said Alice. "And I'm afraid I can't help you much. I gave away my late father's things after he died."

At this point Alice's sister appeared, walking slowly across the dark farmyard toward the barn.

"I found your shoes, Mr. Swift," she said. "That critter, that gollywhopper, must have dropped them in the road. But the rest of your clothes are gone for good, it seems. Whatever will you do now?"

"Well, to tell you the truth, I'm flat broke at the moment, and fresh out of bright ideas. All I have left are my shoes and my good name."

"You could stay here and work on the farm for a while," said the sister. "Harvest time next month. Earn a few dollars, pay Alice back, and then be on your way."

"But what will I wear for clothes?" asked Wiley. "A burlap sack from the hayloft?"

"Why no," said the sister. "We can do you better than that. Alice and I are both pretty clever with a needle and thread."

So Wily Swift sat in the barn for several hours, hungry and full of vague suspicions, while the two women sewed together some clothes for him. The only material they had to spare was a white bed sheet—enough for a shirt, a pair of trousers, and some underwear. That afternoon, they gave Wily his new outfit and sent him out to earn his keep, picking blackberries on the hillside. Once he settled down, he was a good worker.

Watching him from the back porch, Alice smiled as she talked contentedly with her sister.

"You know, dressed all in white, that Mr. Wily Swift looks like a great big gollywhopper at a distance."

"That's just what I was thinking, Alice," her sister replied. "What I was thinking exactly."

Giant Catfish

Lucy Ann Gregorian's family moved from Atlantic City, New Jersey, to Lake Okatibbee, Mississippi, because her father thought it might be the best place to fulfill his lifelong ambition of catching a giant catfish. He was an automobile mechanic by trade, so he could find work almost anywhere, and he shrugged off his wife's worries about not knowing anybody in the rural South.

"People are people," he insisted, "just like cars are cars. This time next year, mark my words, Lucy Ann will be president of her class at school, and you'll be running the P.T.A. or the debating society or whatever takes your fancy."

Lucy Ann, aged eight, liked the school at first. Her father helped her prepare for "Show and Tell." Other third graders brought little things to talk about—a lizard, a bird's egg, some coins from Mexico—but Lucy Ann had a giant catfish. At least she had a *picture* of one. When she showed it to her class, however, the other children mostly laughed and jeered.

"That ain't no giant catfish."

"Maybe it's a catfish, but it couldn't be that big."

Even her teacher was skeptical. "I'm sure you wouldn't deliberately tell us a falsehood, Lucy Ann, but did you say your daddy actually photographed a fish as big as that?"

"No, ma'am," Lucy Ann replied, with some heat. "I said my father *bought* this picture from a man who said *he* took it in Lake Okatibbee. That's why we moved here from New Jersey."

During recess, most of the children avoided Lucy Ann, but one little girl from Japan, named Ryoko, came over and smiled in a friendly way.

"Japanese islands have many such giant catfish," she said.

"Really?" Lucy Ann exclaimed.

"Yes, indeed," Ryoko continued.

"My father wants to catch one," said Lucy Ann.

The two girls strolled pleasantly around the playground, talking about their families and the places they had lived before.

A week later, Lucy Ann's father announced that he was ready to try catching some giant catfish in Lake Okatibbee. On Saturday afternoon, a crowd of adults and children gathered at the edge of the lake to watch. Several newspapers sent reporters and photographers as well.

Lucy Ann's father backed his tow truck down the concrete ramp that was used for launching boats. He had two hundred feet of braided steel cable on his winch, and a large hook, to which he attached a net containing dozens of watermel-  ons. Someone had told him this was one of the giant catfish's favorite foods.

He pushed a lever forward. Slowly the steel cable unwound. The netful of watermelons slid down the ramp and disappeared under water. Gradually the crowd edged closer, but nothing happened. Children began to get restless.

"Told you there was no such thing," one yelled at Lucy Ann.

"Nothin' but turtles in this lake," another said.

Then the steel cable became taut from something pulling on it. The tow truck started sliding backwards down the ramp into the water. Lucy Ann's father gave the motor some more gas. The truck inched forward, and the lake bubbled and churned as though a volcano was about to erupt from the depths. Several people waded in for a closer look. Harder and harder the tow truck pulled. Suddenly a huge dark thing came bursting out of the lake—not a giant catfish but a snapping turtle bigger than an automobile! It gripped the netful of watermelons in its mighty jaws.

When people saw what it was, they laughed and walked away. Lucy Ann held her mother's hand. Her father ran after a photographer.

"I'll pay you to take some pictures," he said.

"Okay, but you won't win any prizes for this here turtle," the photographer answered. "Folks in Lake Okatibbee throw 'em back if they're as small as this one."

Lucy Ann was almost ready to cry.

"Does this mean there's really no such thing as a giant catfish?" she asked.

"Maybe it does, maybe it doesn't," said her father. "But I can't wait to send these turtle photos to the folks back home in New Jersey."

The Jumping Frog of Angel's Camp

Harry Harlow's uncle gave him a twenty dollar gold coin for his twentieth birthday, in 1868, and promptly bet him twenty dollars that it would rain before morning. Harry had never gambled before, but he had a nose for eastern Pennsylvania weather. He stuck his head out the window, sniffed the night air, accepted the bet, and won. Instead of spending his forty dollars he put them aside, and when he took a ship from Philadelphia to San Diego the following year, he made bets with other passengers for amusement. How many miles would they travel in a day? Who would see the next manatee or porpoise? Which seagull would take off first from the afterdeck? Harry bet on all sorts of things, and he won more often than he lost.

By the time he reached California, Harry had such a tidy bundle of banknotes in his innermost pocket that he didn't need the banking job another uncle had offered him by mail. Betting once or twice a day could bring in enough money and leave him with hours of free time to see the sights, make new friends, read a book, or just let his mind wander while he looked at the latest magazines and newspapers.

In San Diego, however, Harry's luck was not as good as it had been on the ship. He lost more bets than he won. Sometimes he would deliberately switch sides—betting *against* his own hunches, as though he could force his luck to change—but that usually didn't succeed either. Harry found that he was running out of money. Even worse, as the word got around that he was becoming desperate, Harry started running out of people to bet with.

"Folks don't like the smell of a loser," an older gambler advised him, "even if it means they'll win."

"What should I do?" Harry asked.

"Try some other places. How about Northern California? Sacramento, for instance. Change the scenery and maybe your luck will change."

Harry pawned his gold watch, bought a horse, and rode towards Sacramento, winning a few bets in each of the little towns along the way. When he got there, however, he grew reckless, betting all of his money on a silver miner whose claim proved to be worthless the next day. Cleaned out—except for his clothes, his horse, and two dollars in change—Harry bet that the horse would *lose* a race against a big green frog. He cheated for the first time in his life, giving his horse so much water to drink that it could hardly move. But the frog couldn't move at all. Harry later discovered that the frog's owner had filled its belly with lead shotgun pellets. So Harry was left with nothing but an idea.

Frogs were plentiful around Sacramento, and jumping contests were easy to organize. Never betting more than a few dollars at a time, Harry secretly loaded his own frog with small pebbles, which could be dumped out after the contest when nobody was looking. He won a lot of greenbacks betting against this poor creature. With his earnings, he bought another horse, a really fast one, and after each successful bet he hopped into the saddle and rode quickly away. Losers sometimes chased him, but he was never caught.

When the time came to leave Sacramento, Harry headed for the mountains. He had heard about rich miners in the Sierra Nevadas. Copper, silver, gold—Harry wasn't sure what they mined, but he knew they had to have money there. Feeling that his luck was going to change once more, Harry stopped at a place called Angel's Camp. This time he organized just one huge contest with very high stakes, and bet every dollar he had against his own immovable frog. As usual, Harry won.

The hardworking miners of Angel's Camp were good sports about losing so much. They carried Harry's winnings for him—four heavy sacks of gold and silver—and helped him to load his saddle bags. Harry swung eagerly into the saddle, but the horse could hardly move. Suddenly there was a loud shout from the big gambling tent where he had left his frog, and Harry knew the game was up.

Leaping out of the saddle, Harry raced to the nearby woods. Nobody chased him because he had nothing left. Weeks later he turned up in San Diego again, a much more thoughtful young man than his uncle had been expecting. They had lunch in a dark-paneled room overlooking the Pacific.

"I bet you'll enjoy banking," his uncle said, but Harry only smiled.

Fur-Bearing Trout

A lot of people go looking for gold, and some of them find it, but some don't—they have to settle for other things, such as the lead that was accidentally discovered among the hills of Colorado in 1877. A group of would-be gold miners decided to become lead miners instead. They named their new community Leadville, and made a decent living for several years. Lead had all sorts of industrial uses in those days, including the bullets that a few of these miners fired harmlessly out of their six-shooters on Saturday nights.

Things were going pretty well until the lead miners got word that twenty-four young ladies from Chicago were going to put on a special show of singing, dancing, and acrobatic exercises at a theatre in Denver the following month. *For Two Days Only*, the notice said. *Tickets $5.00 Each, Box Seats $10.00 Per Head. Lower Prices If Bald.* Denver was only ninety miles away, and most of the miners hadn't seen a pretty girl in two or three years, so they decided to close down the mine for a week and have fun. But they thought they needed some "citified" clothes to dress up in.

That problem was solved the next day, when a traveling salesman appeared at the mining camp. He displayed a full range of finery, from green plaid suits and fancy yellow shoes to red silk neckties and English mustache wax. He even had a liquid called "Patented Hair Subtractor" which was guaranteed to make people bald, for two dollars a bottle.

"Sure it's high-priced," the salesman agreed. "But this is the only product that will take hair off, painlessly and permanently, or you get your money back."

So each and every one of the lead miners bought this liquid, used it, lost their hair, and rode into Denver a few weeks later, wearing their new clothes. They found half a dozen busy theatres, and quite a few young ladies who might have been experts at song, dance, and acrobatics—but not the special ones they were looking for. Disappointed, they rode all the way back to Leadville in gloomy silence. Their gloom deepened when they discovered that the cash-box had been stolen from the lead mine in their absence.

It took the miners nearly a year to earn back the money they had lost through robbery and deception. During that time they experimented with various liquids that promised to restore their hair, but none of these formulas worked. Then a miner named Marcus Galeena had to go home to New York City because his mother was seriously ill. There he heard about a new "scientific" liquid that had supposedly grown hair on a bald gorilla at the Bronx Zoo. It was mighty expensive, twenty-five dollars per gallon, but Marcus had been shown the results by a friend of his cousin's nephew, and he assumed the other miners would pay for some. So he counted out a hundred dollars and started the long journey back to Leadville.

After leaving the train in Denver, Marcus rode through the rolling hills with four big glass jugs of *Hairzup* tied behind his saddle. He was more than halfway to camp when the horse's foot slipped on a log bridge crossing the Tarryall River. Two of the jugs fell off, breaking on the rocks and spilling their contents into the stream. But he still had two gallons left.

"You try it first," the other miners told him. "If it works for you, maybe we'll use it, too."

So Marcus followed the printed instructions exactly, putting *Hairzup* on his skull every eight hours, and wearing his hat day and night to keep the results a secret. Two months later he got dressed up in his citified suit and rode off towards Denver to visit a friend. As he crossed the Tarryall River he looked down, stopped, and got off his horse. The stream was full of strange fish. Trout, they looked like, but trout covered with black fur!

Marcus got an idea.

He staked a claim to 160 acres along the river, built some comfortable cabins, and advertised in the Eastern newspapers. Hunters and fishermen came from far and wide to try their luck with *Fur-Bearing Trout*. They did all right, but the fish kept multiplying, and Marcus kept making money. He built a really comfortable cabin for himself on nearby Bald Mountain. From there he smiled down at the world, though he never did grow much hair.

Groundhog Sees His Shadow

Mike Cornelius joined the Navy in 1928, following his eighteenth birthday, because he wanted to travel around the world. After training he was assigned to weather forecasting on a brand new cruiser, but it was peacetime, and his ship never sailed from Pearl Harbor, Hawaii, to any of the other places he had imagined. So he took his pay at the end of four years and went home to Punxsutawney, a small town about halfway down the road between Pittsburgh, Pennsylvania, and nowhere in particular.

Arriving on a beautiful October day, Mike was shocked to find stores out of business, streets deserted, "For Sale" signs on houses. His father, who ran the local newspaper, looked tired and discouraged as they sat in the office.

"What's happening, Dad?" Mike asked.

"You've been away too long," his father replied. "We're having what they call a Depression. Twenty percent unemployment, closer to thirty percent out here in the boondocks—and things are getting worse instead of better."

Mike wanted to ask some questions, but the look on his father's face told him it was time to shut up, so he left the newspaper office and walked slowly along Punxsutawney's main street. People passed him with their heads down. Almost nobody seemed to recognize him. By the time he reached the end of the sidewalk and started back, Mike was feeling depressed himself.

"I can't stand this," he thought. "I've got to do something about it."

After supper, Mike talked with his father again.

"This town needs a gimmick," he suggested.

"A what?" his father asked.

"A gimmick, a special thing, to make us stand out. One of my shipmates told me about it. He's from Brooklyn."

"How about a baseball team, like the Dodgers?"

They both laughed, and kicked around a few more ideas, but nothing special occurred to them.

"Punxsutawney has one gimmick I can think of," Mike's father said finally, "the worst winters in Pennsylvania. See what you can do with that."

The next morning Mike walked two miles out of town to visit his best friend, Bud Weder, who had taken up farming right after high school.

"How bad have the winters been lately?" Mike asked.

"Well, last year the snow was higher than the barn door for two months," Bud said. "I had to dig a tunnel to get hay out to my cows. The only critter that seemed happy about the weather was an old groundhog."

"What old groundhog?" said Mike.

"The one that lives up there on the hill. He don't care how deep the snow gets. He just digs his way out and dances around like a kid at a birthday party."

"Show me."

Bud led Mike to the hilltop, where a dead elm tree stood by itself. He pointed to the hole between its roots.

"That's where he lives, but you won't see him until the weather is real bad."

Mike returned to the groundhog's hole in late December, when it snowed all day. He waited patiently. Just before dark he heard the sound of digging. Then a head appeared, covered with spiky brown fur. Gleaming eyes scanned the hilltop, noticed Mike, ignored him. Teeth showed in a grin. Mike retreated to the edge of the hill and watched the old groundhog emerge, stretch, and do a little dance. Wet snow was falling thickly now, but Mike felt happy for the first time in months.

By February the snow was six feet deep, so Mike's father printed a story complete with photographs of the dancing groundhog. It caused a big stir in Punxsutawney and beyond. The mayor called him immediately, hoping for a miracle.

"Let me get this straight, now," said the mayor. "If our groundhog *doesn't* see his shadow, we'll have six more weeks of winter?"

"No, the other way around," Mike's father explained. "If he *does* see his shadow, we'll have six more weeks of winter."

"Is this some kind of scientific discovery, do you think?"

"I'm afraid not," Mike's father chuckled. "It's really just some kind of a gimmick."

Crook-Jaw the Whale

In 1690 the island of Nantucket was struck by a tremendous hurricane—the worst storm that anybody could remember. Starting on a Saturday morning, the sky became darker and darker. Trees, sheds, fences were swept away as the wind blew harder and harder. People took shelter in their houses, but soon the yards were filled with blowing sand. Feeling trapped, some managed to get outdoors. What they saw was even more frightening than what they had imagined. Huge waves, driven by the wind, were rolling across beaches and fields. Ugly brown foam swirled through the streets of the town. Wooden docks and several small ships had vanished from the harbor. Half the island was under water, and people feared they were going to be swallowed up by the sea.

Sunday morning the wind stopped blowing, and the waves were much smaller. People gathered on a hilltop, discussing what to do. Some thought the storm was over. Others wanted to escape to the mainland of Massachusetts, thirty miles away, while they had the chance. They approached Nathaniel Oakwood, the captain of a merchant ship that was still afloat in the harbor, and begged him to carry them to safety. But Nathaniel knew the hurricane was only half over, and he wanted to move his ship far away from land, before it could be destroyed. So he summoned his crew, took his wife and children with him, and quickly put to sea.

Two hours later, as the wind picked up again and the waves grew larger, Nathaniel's lookout shouted from the foremast.

"Whale Ho!" he cried, pointing straight ahead.

Nathaniel couldn't spot it at first, but suddenly his ship rose high on a breaking wave and he saw the great head, huge and pale gray, rising to meet him head-on. Broken harpoons hung from the whale's body, and its jaws were twisted into a crooked grin. Nathaniel turned the ship's wheel sharply to avoid a collision, but the whale turned with him and swam closer. Nathaniel turned farther, until his ship was running before the wind. Looking over his shoulder, he saw the big whale just behind. Its crooked jaws were opening, as though to swallow Nathaniel's ship in one bite.

"Jump for your lives!" Nathaniel yelled.

He cut the lifeboat loose and watched his family and crew swim towards it. As soon as they were safe, he spun the ship around again and sailed it straight into the open jaws of the oncoming whale, where it stuck like a cork in the mouth of a bottle.

"Try feeding on this!" Nathaniel shouted.

He meant to jump to safety then, but the whale's jaws closed with a loud crunch! Nathaniel was trapped inside. The whale began chewing on pieces of wood and can-  vas. When it swallowed, Nathaniel started sliding down a long smooth throat, two feet deep in water. Towards the bottom a light appeared, and Nathaniel thought he could hear voices.

"I must be dreaming," he said to himself, "or maybe I'm dead."

But when Nathaniel reached the bottom of the whale's gullet, he found himself in a round white chamber, mysteriously lighted. Two peo- ple were sitting at a table, playing cards. One was a young woman with glowing red hair and a disarming smile. The other, wearing horns and a tail, appeared to be the Devil. Afterwards, Nathaniel couldn't remember exactly what they talked about, but the general notion was that the woman wanted to marry him—and the Devil would perform the ceremony.

Nathaniel refused and the woman wept while the Devil became angry. He leaped up from his chair to wrestle with Nathaniel. He was very strong, and Nathaniel would probably have lost that fight, but suddenly the whale must have burped from eating too much too fast. Nathaniel was suddenly thrown upward, into the whale's mouth. He squeezed between those terrible jaws, dived into the sea, and swam to a floating crate from which he was rescued three days later.

When Nathaniel's wife heard his story, she tried to persuade him to retire from the sea.

"There are too many hazards, my love," she said.

"But I'm not a whaler," Nathaniel insisted. "I'll never run into that wicked old Crook-Jaw again."

Just to make sure, Nathaniel's wife got him a special harpoon for the next voyage. It had a very sharp point of solid silver, which was designed to pierce the Devil's heart in any of his disguises.

Rawhide Railroad

Doc Baker wanted to build a short railroad from Walla Walla to Wallula, back in the 1880s, but most people didn't take him seriously. Easterners thought he was talking about Hawaii, and they didn't see a need for train service there. Westerners got the general idea—carrying timber from the immense forests of Washington and Oregon, down to the Columbia River and the sawmills—but the practical difficulties seemed so great that even Doc's best friends doubted if a railroad could actually be built.

"It's only thirty miles, as the crow flies," Doc would say, and his pals would just grin at one another. Railroads didn't have wings!

Doc was well aware of the problems he faced. His railroad had to go through Indian country, and the Chinooks might oppose it. There wasn't a locomotive or a flatcar available within a thousand miles. Even the steel rails would have to be shipped in from Pittsburgh, Pennsylvania, then carried overland by mules. Only the iron spikes could be made locally. And the ties, of course—there was plenty of wood for making railroad ties, as trees were cut to clear the way for the tracks.

Last but not least, Doc needed to borrow money. In desperation, he called upon an eighty-year-old widow, Mrs. Wrangell, whose husband had struck gold in Alaska.

"I'll put up every dollar of the money you need," said she, "on three conditions. Number one, you get the railroad running by Christmas. Two, I want to drive the first train. And three, there'll be no hunting of animals on this railway line—no elk, no bears, not even a bow-legged beaver. Agreed?"

Doc agreed—he would have agreed to almost anything at that moment. From Portland, Oregon, he telegraphed a railroad company near Los Angeles, California, and arranged to buy a small locomotive and ten old flatcars for cash. He also sent telegrams to the rail-making factory in Pittsburgh but got no reply. Then he canoed up the river to the Chinook fishing village, where the chief was slow to accept him.

"Our people need work, but must be sure no hunting on railroad."

Doc talked with Mrs. Wrangell, and made a deal to hire two hundred Chinook warriors to guard the railroad right-of-way from anything that might threaten it. The chief wanted to drive the first train, but settled for blowing the whistle as it approached the curves, with Mrs. Wrangell driving.

A month later, Doc's locomotive and flatcars were being unloaded from a ship in Portland. Lumbermen had cut and trimmed thousands of wooden ties for the railroad. Blacksmiths had forged the iron spikes. Still missing were the steel rails for the tracks, and Doc was going crazy—the factory back in Pittsburgh had permanently closed!

Doc's foreman suggested making rails out of wood, which was all they had. Doc hesitated, but what else could he do? Wooden rails were cut to size, laid on ties, and spiked down like steel ones. When the first train started rolling along the track in December, with Mrs. Wrangell driving and the chief standing by, Doc held his breath—the rails worked.

"I'd take it kind of slow," the foreman advised.

Gradually the wooden rails splintered and cracked, and Doc couldn't find steel to replace them. The chief of the Chinooks proposed to cover them with rawhide—leather so tough that almost nothing could make a dent in it. His people did the job for pay, and the rails worked just fine. Train loads of timber were moved. Doc paid back the money he had borrowed from Mrs. Wrangell and started thinking about new ideas to develop.

But it snowed heavily in early March, and the tracks had to be shoveled by hand every day. Grass, bushes, and small trees were covered with huge snowdrifts. Cattle couldn't graze, wild animals starved, and hungry wolves came close to the tracks. Soon the wolves were chewing the rawhide rails!

"Can't hardly blame the poor critters," Doc's foreman said. "Nothing else to eat."

Doc didn't know what to do. Mrs. Wrangell wouldn't let him shoot the wolves, and the Chinooks would have torn up his tracks if he had. Then somebody sent a lot of sweet molasses up to Walla Walla by mistake. It leaked all over the tracks, and the wolves learned to like it better than rawhide, so they stopped chewing on the rails, and licked them clean. Knowing where to get plenty of molasses at a low price, Doc went right ahead and ordered more.

Daniel Boone Met His Wife
While Chasing Deer

Daniel Boone was born in Berks County, Pennsylvania, around 1740. He grew up tall and strong, loving the outdoors, hating to be inside, going to school when he had to, fishing in the river and creeks, hunting as often as he could.

Hunting was what he called it, but usually he was just scaring the game. Daniel's father had given him a flintlock musket to learn with, telling him that he had to eat anything he killed. As this old weapon was very inaccurate, Daniel fired harmlessly at rabbits, squirrels, and turkeys. He seldom hit what he meant to, but he gradually realized that he was farsighted. Distant things were sharp and clear to him. Up close, things could become blurry and somewhat unreal.

When Daniel was thirteen, his family moved to North Carolina, near the Tennessee border. Daniel took to the woods, wearing buckskins and moccasins like an Indian, so he could run swiftly and silently. He was given a long rifle, and it was his job to put meat on the table. Easy to do. There was so much game that he spent more and more of his time hunting for pleasure.

Bears became his specialty—big, fast, smart, and dangerous animals. Daniel would roam the Blue Ridge, tracking them until he was close enough to make one turn around and face him. Using a knife or just his bare hands, Daniel would growl with joy and fight to the death. Sooner or later, his great strength and his fast reflexes

188

would prevail. Then he would carve his name on a nearby tree—proudly, though he never told his father about it.

Deer were different—fast, but neither smart nor dangerous. No challenge. Daniel hunted them with a friend, using the technique known as "shining the eyes." He would run ahead, carrying a pan full of blazing pine knots, into the thickets where deer lay hidden. Often a startled animal would leap up, blinded, dazed by the bright light. Then it would freeze. Daniel's friend would shoot. *Bang!* And another deer was ready for the boys to carry home.

Daniel didn't tell his father about this kind of hunting, either, because he felt vaguely that it was wrong. Yet it was quick and almost certain, leaving him free to go after bear or cougar or sometimes mountain lion. So he continued for more than four years, until the night before his eighteenth birthday, when his friend was sick and Daniel had to get a deer by himself.

Carrying his lighted fire pan in one hand, Daniel ran easily along, ducking under low branches, ready to shoot if he saw a deer's eyes shining back at him. But he stumbled suddenly on a fallen tree, and the fire pan rolled away. As he groped for it, the pan seemed to come towards him, and Daniel was blinded by the light. He was surprised, momentarily confused. The bright light moved closer. Daniel stood up, forgetting his rifle and backing off. The fire pan followed! Daniel felt deep fear—mindless, stomach-clenching fear—which he had never felt before. He turned and ran, with the fire pan close behind.

As fast as he went, Daniel couldn't escape from this frightening thing—until he heard a gasp, a shriek, a crash when the fire pan hit the ground. He turned. There in the light of the embers, Daniel thought he saw a girl dressed in buckskins like himself—white or Indian he couldn't tell—dark hair down to her waist. She whispered something, then she turned and fled.

Daniel chased her through the moonlit forest, crossing the ridge line after midnight, plunging down into dark valleys on the western side. Running, running, Daniel felt his lungs about to burst. Ahead he heard the girl gasping too, but there were clouds across the moon and he could no longer see her.

Finally they came to a long field of corn, with log cabins beyond. Now the girl seemed to have turned into a deer! Shots rang out from the cabins. Lights. Daniel stopped. He felt different. Puzzled, he looked at himself and saw that he too was a deer! He raced back to the shelter of the trees. Rested. Listened. Heard a slight rustling sound nearby. Felt a cool snout touch his snout. Knew who it was. Felt his heart surge. Knew that he would marry her as soon as she became a girl again. Knew that he would run with her whenever she was a deer. Turned, and followed her away from there.

Other Tales of Incredible Animals

Animals that talk occasionally, or make themselves understood in other ways, contribute to a steady stream of humor in American folk tales. For instance, there was the horse that went into a restaurant in Cheyenne, Wyoming, and ordered a hot fudge sundae with horseradish on top. The person behind the counter made no comment but simply started working on the order, which surprised the horse. "Don't you think it's kind of unusual for a horse to do that?" the horse asked. "Not at all," was the reply. "Lots of my customers like horseradish with their ice cream."

An Arkansas farmer made his hired man stay up all night to find out who or what was stealing his corn. It turned out to be a big old bear, which chased the hired man around and around the corn crib. After a dozen laps, the hired man was able to grab the bear's tail and hang on—that way the bear couldn't quite catch him. Next morning the farmer came out, saw what was happening, and took the hired man's place for a spell. But the hired man went home, fell asleep, and didn't return. Finally the bear grew tired of the chase and called for a time out. Being pretty tired himself, the farmer agreed. So the bear and the farmer rested side by side for a couple of hours before they got up and went at it again.

Other tall tales involve animals that have something unbelievable happen to them. For example, "Old Lightning" was an Alabama hound dog capable of outrunning just about anything on legs until he had a bad accident—he ran smack into a sawmill and split himself down the middle. His owner quickly put the two halves back together, but got confused and did it wrong. From then on the left side of that poor dog tried to run forward while the right side could only run backward.

The people of Windham, Connecticut, led such quiet lives that they normally went to bed after supper and slept through to sunrise or later. One night in 1758 some strange noises awakened them—thumping, bumping, and what sounded like deep voices speaking a language they hadn't heard before. Fearing an invasion by the French or the Indians, with whom their British government was at war, they fled. Later they found that the "invaders" were actually thousands of ordinary green frogs taking the shortest route through town from New Haven to Providence, Rhode Island, for reasons still unknown.

A Japanese-American boy named Momotaro was determined to follow the customs of his ancestors, even though he lived in the Nevada desert thousands of miles from Japan. At age eighteen he went forth to find and conquer the hideous monsters known as *oni,* which had preyed upon his people for countless generations. As he approached the mountains where he thought the *oni* might be lurking, young Momotaro was joined by three good animals—Lord Dog, Lord Monkey, and Lord Pheasant. With their assistance he defeated so many *oni* in combat that the others retreated into their secret caverns and did not bother people again for many years.

Real snakes can be scary, but snakes in folk tales are usually no match for the cleverness or strength of the main characters. They get tied in knots, cut into pieces, tranquilized by magical music, or otherwise rendered harmless. An exception was the buckhorn snake, fifteen feet long, wearing big black horns like an antelope. Chased by this creature, a hunter ran all the way from the Canadian border down to Bismarck, North Dakota, where he took refuge in a barber shop, his hair still standing on end. He had to have three haircuts, one after another, before he looked normal again.

A hiker got lost in the Maine woods on a cold winter day, and decided to climb a very tall tree. High in its leafless branches he could see snow-brushed Mount Katahdin in the distance and the frozen shape of Pemadumcook Lake in the opposite direction, so he figured out which way to go. As he started to climb down, the tree shook itself and rose up from the ground. Terrified, the hiker realized that he was riding the antlers of an enormous deer, which had been sound asleep until that very moment. It raced off through the forest with great leaps and bounds, but let the hiker down gently on a logging trail he recognized, and soon he was home.

A little girl named Gretchen was traveling to Texas with her family in 1848. Riding on top of the overloaded wagon while her parents walked alongside, she was carried off across the prairie when the horses saw a rattlesnake and bolted. Hours later she encountered a herd of wild mares with a magnificent white stallion in their midst. The stallion bit through the harness on Gretchen's wagon to set the horses free, then came close to her and stood quietly as she climbed onto his back. Faster than the wind, he returned her safely to her parents, who were so upset about Gretchen's disappearance and the loss of their horses and wagon that they scarcely noticed how she had been rescued.

Finally, there are some folk animals so unbelievable that they can't be described —they have to be imagined by the reader. These unlikely critters include slide-rock bolters, swallow oysters, sky foogles, ganninippers, and bald-headed whizzers, not to mention occasional appearances by the cactus cat, the splinter cat, the squonk, the billdad, or even the tripodero.

A wonderful assortment of incredible animals, among many other kinds of folk characters, can be found in B. A. Botkin's *Treasury of American Folklore.* Regional collections are also worth searching for, such as Joseph Bruchack's *Hoop Snakes, Hide Behinds and Side-Hill Winders,* or Harvey Carr's *I Was on the Wrong Bear,* for tales of the Adirondacks.